26
DEGREES
BELOW

20
DEGREES
BELOW

26 DEGREES BELOW

THROUGH HELL AND BACK

Scott V.L. Mack

26 DEGREES BELOW
THROUGH HELL AND BACK

iUniverse books may be ordered through booksellers or by contacting:

iUniverse
1663 Liberty Drive
Bloomington, IN 47403
www.iuniverse.com
844-349-9409

ISBN: 978-1-6632-0357-1 (sc)
ISBN: 978-1-6632-0358-8 (e)

Library of Congress Control Number: 2024924566

Print information available on the last page.

iUniverse rev. date: 01/20/2025

CHARACTERS

Casey

Retired CIA Agent
Reinstated do to Red Dawn Plot
Son of Retired District Attorney
Bella of Washington DC
Speaks different languages
Meditates/Morning Jogger
Has A Secret Love Interest

Casey (retired CIA)

TRACY

CIA Secretary
(Walter Little sister)

Entered the United States Federal
Witness Protection Program, also known
as the Witness Security Program,
or WITSEC

Tracy Fletcher (CIA paper pusher)

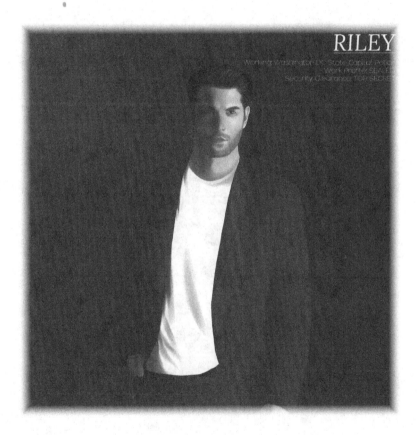

RILEY
Working: Washington DC State Capitol Police
Work Profile: SEALED
Security Clearance: TOP SECRET

Riley (local detective)

Walter (deceased)

Big Ronnie (Italian mafia)

Dimitri (Russian mafia)

Aaron "Left hand" Blaze (Boston Mafia)

CHASE

Married to Miller's Daughter (Alexa)
Chase is Retired Delta Force
Now working for THE U.S. as an CIA Agent
Chase Speaks Five Different Languages
Expecting 1st Child
Parents: UNKNOWN

Chase (agent 1)

Bella (Casey mother)

Joe (Barber)

Brandon (Arms dealer)

Stella (money laundering)

Miller (Boss from Langley)

Angelica Hernandez Garcia (Pastel Hernandez sister)

Pastel Hernandez

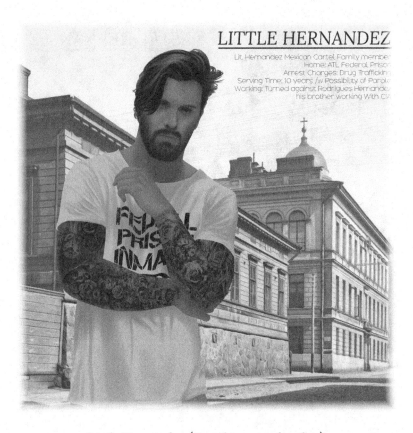

LITTLE HERNANDEZ

Lit. Hernandez Mexican Cartel Family member
Home: ATL Federal Prison
Arrest Charges: Drug Trafficking
Serving Time; 10 years /w Possibility of Parole
Working: Turned against Rodrigues Hernandez
his brother working With CIA

Little Hernandez (Pastel younger brother)

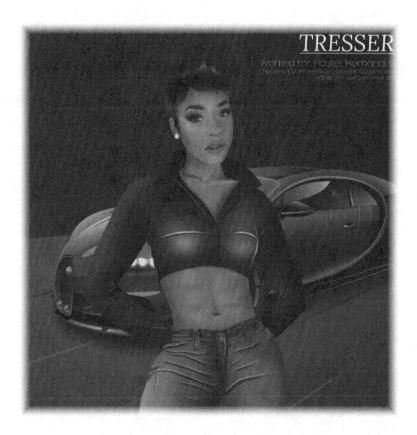

Tresser (CIA Informer)

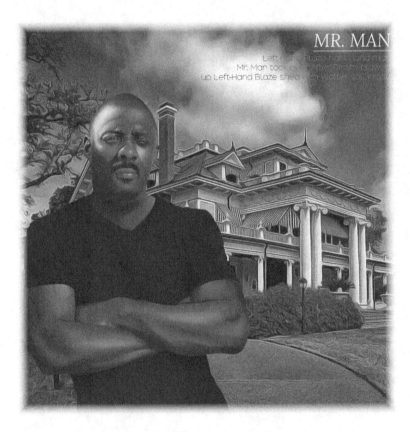

Mr. Man (working for Blaze)

Val (NSA)

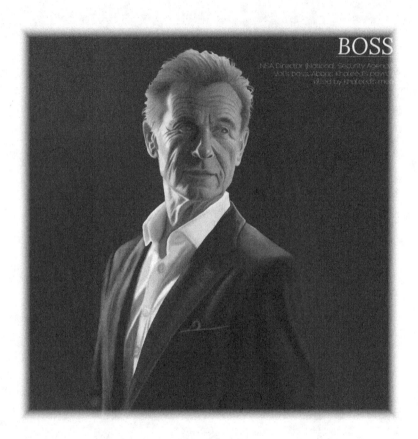

BOSS
NSA Director (National Security Agency)
Val's boss, Abbas Khaleed's payroll
killed by khaleed's men

Boss (NSA)

LAWYER

Name: Vincenzo Lee Joong
Replacing 1st Lawyer
Viktor's Mafia Lawyer
Hired to Defend Dimitri on Treason & Fraud

Lawyer (working for the Russian Kingpin Mafia/ deceased)

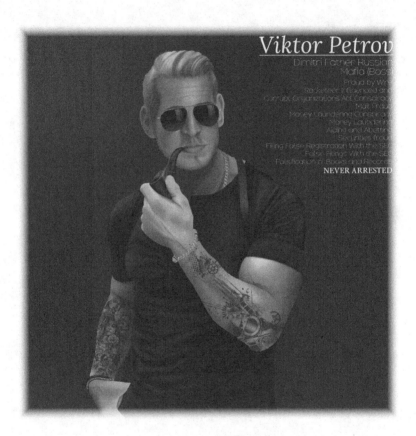

Viktor Petrov (Dimitri Father)

MICHELLE
Government agent
(unknown department)
Black market- last chance
Chase cousin

Michelle (Chase's cousin)

PROLOGUE

Miller summoned Casey out of retirement. Red Dawn was becoming a Death sentence. The CIA needed help from one of their former agents from back in his day, Casey, who always came through. They needed to bring him out of retirement to help them out with the Red Dawn case. Miller remembered him and Casey slicing bodies and running through flying bullets like the old days. A friendship is formed in a new partner who goes by the name of Chase, a former Delta Force highly classified agent. Big Ronnie and Left-hand Blaze are small time Mafia that tries to branch out in the big league.

Blaze purchased stolen weapons off Dimitri. Later, Blaze realized he needed someone to demonstrate the stolen weapons he had purchased. Dimitri volunteered to show a demonstration with each auction purchase. He was willing to risk entering the United States even after he had been placed on the CIA red alert border list. He entered American soil hired by Blaze to help out with the stolen weapon and to exhibit the weapons on a live auction. They sold these weapons throughout the syndicate world.

Getting these explosives out of Russia came with a price. Dimitri tried to ship fifteen explosives to the US that were purchased by Blaze. Somehow the government found out and sent in two of the CIA's best agents surging through Russia along with other field agents that specialized in problem solving. Chase and Casey got ambushed in the process of taking the weapons that were stolen in the first place from the US Government. Chase and Casey where only able to get twelve out of those fifteen explosives before they left Russian soil.

The bad guys figured out a way and were able to get away with three that made their way into the US. Miller needed someone that was going to get the job done after Chase was reassigned and sent to Afghanistan on another case. Casey was left behind to clean up the Governments' mess. Even though Casey was working Red Dawn case alone, Chase would always call giving him valuable information to help him along the way. After all that, Casey thought Chase was part of the reason why the three weapons made it over to American soil. Casey found out that Chase was a true friend.

On their mission, going through different parts of the world trying to bring in Dimitri for treason, Casey ran into Tresser in Ukraine. Casey and Chase went down in a plane crash, with the pilot and crew, in the urban and wooded area of Ukraine. Along the way Tresser ended up being a treader. Tresser was working with Dimitri, and they were trying to dismantle Casey's credibility with a lot of mayhem. Trading sides, Tresser held Dimitri hostage for one Pastel Hernandez, Mexican Cartel, before turning him over. She gave Dimitri the ass whipping of his life. Later, she found out that she was just Pastel's little patsy.

Chase and Casey traveled from American soil to Romania, Budapest, Russia, Norway, Finland, Savannah Georgia, and even Atlanta Georgia. They were looking for the CIA's most wanted, Dimitri Petrov along with Patel Hernandez. The hunt became a mission that was not impossible.

"You will never be bored; I promise this book is filled with breathtaking, adventurous situations. Written with cockiness and dangerous characters but also with plenty of bold, daring risk taking situations with some minor explicit language."

CHAPTER ONE

Red Dawn

The Pentagon of Washington, DC.

THE UNITED STATES General walks into the briefing room where he was saluted by lower-ranking officers. He goes directly to the center of the room, which is filled with military computer technicians, and he faces the big screen.

"Give me a satellite view of our convoy, please!"

Technician types in the coordinates.

As they enter coordinates into the system, the convoy shows up on the satellite traveling through the Syrian Desert.

"You now have the view, Sir."

"Someone get me Captain Sanders on the comms right… … … NOW!"

Capt. Sanders answers the call.

{"Sir."}

"Captain Richard Sanders, this is the United States Army General. I am assuming you know who I am."

{"Yes Sir!"}

"I was debriefed this morning on a separate line from the United States. There will not be any further delays with assignment of the allocated destination that are being led by your troops who are in your command to transport America's artillery of the 15 missiles. The mission is to make sure the package arrives safely to its' destination!"

{"Sir, Yes Sir."}

"Good luck and a safe journey."

Meanwhile, a man sits on his camel watching the United States military convoy traveling through the desert through a pair of binoculars. After spotting the military convoy, he counts seven military units riding right behind each other in a straight line. He signals another man using a glass-like object for flashing to another man, like Morse code. Then the man that got the flashing signal calls in the attack.

Back at the Pentagon, one of the technicians calls out to the General once he sees the satellite picking up strange activities from an unknown source.

"Sir?"

The General turns around to look at the screen.

"Call Off the Operation!"

Before they could act, an enemy sniper caught Captain Sander as the bullet pierced through the front windshield. The shot went through and through the captain's head as the driver of the hummer swerves. The vehicle loses traction causing it to flip three times. The convoy comes to a halt as they get into defense mode. Two men approach the flipped vehicle to check for any sign of life from the captain and the driver. One of the soldiers checks for a pulse.

"No pulse, they're gone!"

The soldiers hear a helicopter in their immediate vicinity.

In the meantime, back at the Pentagon

"Get these men some air support now!"

The American soldiers realize that the aircraft they spotted were not Americans. They realized an unmarked black helicopter was coming their way with attached machine guns on each side. One of the soldiers' yells:

"TAKE COVER!"

As the soldiers ran for cover, the helicopter opens fire taking out three men as the remaining opens fire at the chopper. An unmarked military truck comes from the side of the convoy. The remaining soldiers surrender while the enemies unload the missiles. The explosion causes the ground to tremble as the General, and the rest of the technicians, watches the live feed.

"What is the ETA on air support?"

"45 min."

"We are not going to get there in time!"

The mercenaries open fire on the remaining American convoys.

"My God!"

After the mercenaries finish the sweep, they load the missiles into their vehicle and flees the scene.

"*Keep that satellite on them. I do not want them to escape!*"

Suddenly, the screen went pitch black as a message pop on the screen.

NO SIGNAL.

"*What the hell happened?*"

"*Someone hacked our system, sir.*"

The General walks to the phone to make a call.

"*Sir, we have an issue. Operation Red Dawn has been discovered!*"

NOVEMBER
NEW YORK, NEW YORK

Casey spends his mornings jogging around Central Park, New York. On this cold airy morning, Casey passes two men who seem to be dressed as agents. As he turns in with the motion of his body from the jog, Casey looks back quickly and the men were still behind him. Casey stumbles upon two more men up ahead. He spots Miller sitting down enjoying his hot cup of coffee.

Casey (walks up closer): "*Miller, you know when civilians spot people wearing suits and dark shades, it is never a good sign to the public. Especially when it comes to another agent because we all know they are working for the government!*"

Casey sits next to Miller on the park bench while other agents are keeping the perimeter clear from potential threats around the area.

"*Special Agent Casey retired CIA operative.*"

"*RETIRED CIA OPERATIVE. Now the real question is, why are you here? I have served my time in the field protecting my country.*"

"Red Dawn is why I am here."

"Red Dawn is an easy mission. Director Miller, did your agents mess it up and now you're here for me to clean up your chaos?"

"How about we take a ride?"

"How 'bout we not. Did you not hear me? I AM RETIRED so no more assignments!"

"According to National Security, when the nation has been threatened and it is a time of war and action, we need all operatives, even past ones. You should know that as an agent."

"I am NO James Bond, Miller!"

"Casey, the assignment has been compromised. We are trying to balance out what took place from our homeland. Red Dawn assignment was your mission to start with. Oh, one more thing, your CIA identity has been reinstated and you are no longer retired!"

Agent Miller stands up while folding his newspaper.

"Then I guess we better take that ride huh?"

"It will be just like old times."

Casey, Miller, and the agents approach the end of the park. As they do, four black Chevrolet Tahoe SUVs line up behind one another. More federal agents were approaching, and some were standing by the SUV's protecting the perimeter, as everyone began to load up.

"A bulletin just hit the Washington Pentagon which has now been passed to the CIA."

As Miller hands Casey a vanilla file folder, Casey begins to open the folder while Miller continues to brief him on the case.

"*The United States Army has been moving top-notch explosives from one camp to another. The US was planning on having the merchandise shipped, but the navy vessel never made it. We think the vessel took a direct hit in the middle of nowhere.*"

"*I remember the case. These were not just any explosives. We are talking about missiles that can start a war in any country.*"

"*Of course, not just any War World 3 either. The General and technicians witnessed the attack live!*"

As Casey continues viewing the file, he sees pictures of dead soldiers.

"*They murdered those men execution-style!*"

"*Mercenaries for hire did the attack.*"

"*Any idea who payroll those men were on?*"

"*That is where you come in Casey. We need you out in the field. We are hoping you can blow a hole big enough in this to find out who is behind this massacre. A bulletin has already hit the CIA in Washington, DC and someone is buying explosives from Russia. Casey, Washington is giving you the CIA Red Dawn file. They needed six field agents. All six of those field agents are in New York. You are one of those field agents. Since you have more seniority, I am putting you in charge.*"

All five field agents were flown in on a Blackhawk from New York to Washington, DC. After the briefing, before heading out, they need to gear up on clothing. They were all heading to Chechnya, Russia. 26 degrees felt different from the 26 degrees in New York. They head out to Ireland on a C130. They finish on a Blackhawk, in the middle of the night, near the enemy line. HQ was online through a feed watching what was taking place. An underground bunker is where they are holding the explosive devices that were brought by someone in the US. The government had no proof of who brought the explosives in the US. Before they went in, Casey signaled to the two guys on the back and two guys on the front. Chase, who is a sniper, was 2000 yards away from the bunker in case someone tries to run out. He had that covered from far away.

As Chase looks through his rifle lens, he gets caught off guard by a gun pointed at the back of his head. Before he got up, he swept the ground with his leg. The gunman fell to the ground and Chase fell on top of him using his elbows on his Torso. A lethal head butt fulfilled its destructive potential. Chase was able to obtain his gun from the gunman. As the gunman tried to get back up, Chase butted him in the head with his rifle. Before Chase could get back in position, all hell broke loose.

Casey runs outside after a Russian. Chase had his eyes open and hit him with a bullseye; he went down. Casey felt like it was a setup. He felt like they were waiting on them the minute they hit the ground. Guns and explosives were flying everywhere. An airstrike came in before they could even get their hands on the explosive devices. They flowed in and picked up a medium slender built Russian. That night, two of their best field agents got killed. Casey, Chase, and the other two were the only ones to walk out of there that night. Everything happened so fast with no warning. Their ride came in the middle of the night, dropped a ladder down, and picked them up. The other Blackhawk went in picking up the bodies of the field agents that lost their lives for this mission.

After they reached Ireland, The Directorate of Military Intelligence "DENT" was informed of the men who did not make it. They were taken to the morgue to prepare them for the long flight home. Casey wanted to stay behind and finish the job. Washington got word and was willing to send more men. He wanted to be in charge because no one could be trusted. They notified them back in Washington and Miller made it happen by backing him. The men were coming the next day. He would brief them when they got in.

That evening, they were heading out on a Blackhawk coming into Ingushetia on 6 Tons into the Grozny back road. They got word from the Australian Secret Intelligence Service that the explosives were getting ready to be shipped to the US. They were given the route to an airfield. As Casey's men made it to the airport, before they arrived, his team were able to get set up. As they were coming in, no one knew what hit them. It was a complete success. They were able to conceal the weapons that were heading in the United States. Chase helped Casey with bringing the missiles back into the country.

Chase was puzzled as he was counting. He recounted and something did not add up; three explosives were missing. He walks in to have a talk with Casey. As he walks into the room, Casey was on a satellite conference call with the Director-General of the Australians, the Director of Secret Service in the United States, Secretary of State, and his boss at Langley. Chase walks up to Casey and whispers in his ear. Casey had a confused look on his face. He broke the bad news to the Directors, Secretary of State, and his Boss Miller. He informs them that they could not get all the weapons, and that three were missing, letting them know that these weapons are indeed heading their way.

Miller gave Casey a call on a mainland phone.

Miller [Langley]: *"How bad is it?"*

{"It's terrible. They got a 15-hour head start."}

"Get back here ASAP."

Casey packs his things and he, along with Chase, brings back the bodies of the men that gave their lives for their country. Miller sent a private plane to bring them home. As they both head back to New York in the US, they watch them load in the caskets of their field agents before getting redirected to Langley Virginia CIA Headquarters as they will be taking their place. They reach their destination. The coffins were unloaded, and they headed into the office. They gave a briefing on what took place in Russia. Their boss Miller walks in to tell them that they had gotten word that the weapons already made it to the US. After considering all that, Miller told Casey that he had another assignment for him and that he would give him five field agents. Casey told him that he will need four agents. Chase is the 5th agent.

Casey could not get his head wrapped around the missing explosives. He could not stop thinking about it. He was thinking to himself how they got the three explosive weapons. How did they know they were even there? Who is the buyer of those weapons? It was a mystery because no one knew anything. Before hitting the field, he had time to stop by to visit his mother, Bella. Just as he walks in the kitchen, she hits him in the head.

"Did you wash up because you are all in my pots?"

"Ma, I just tasted a little of what you got on and it smells divine. You know I always loved your cooking. No one can beat your fried chicken, and God forbid your Mac and Cheese."

"Wash up and tell me how work is going."

"You know, selling cameras to these wealthy people is a headache. It is getting kind of hard because people are so cheap these days."

"Well son, you can sell a blind guide dog to a seeing man. You are good at your job so please do not give up!"

His mother takes one look at him.

"If you need anything, let me know!"

"Ma, you raised me right. Now if there is anything you need, let me know."

He spent that evening with Bella, had dinner, then off he went. Casey had not slept in days. All he would do was meditate. He stops by the gym to meditate that night. Everything was running through his mind 100 miles a minute. He was wondering if there was someone on the interior of the agency that is feeding information to the Mafia gang.

Chase wanted to inform Casey that they have a 0400-hour meeting on a video conference call. Casey trained that whole night in the gym. Casey places a call to Tracy Fletcher, CIA paper-pusher, to look in on Chase's background. He just could not wrap his mind around a lot of things that did not make any sense. The next day Tracy Fletcher called Casey with Chase's background check.

"I found out that Chase was Delta Force years ago. He has declassified files, so no one can read his missions, unless you have higher clearance."

"Who is this, Chase? Yeah, it makes you wonder. Tracy, can you keep digging around? See what else you can find out like does he have a wife, kids, anything."

"Sure, thing Casey!"

He is back to square one. The next morning, around 0400 hours after the phone conference, Chase and Casey gather up their things. They had another briefing at Langley. Miller walks in to discuss the whereabouts of the explosives that were missing. The word on the street is that the Mafia is planning something big, and that the Russian Mafia is in the US.

"Miller Sir, do you know which mob family is here from Russia."

"It is Dimitri Petrov. He is here on a Business Visa? Border Control just informed us that he just came through Customs about 0500 hours ago. So, we can only assume that he is here because of those explosives. Dimitri is in New York City. I have a plane waiting for the both of you on the runway right now. I need some answers as of yesterday."

As Chase and Casey left for the airfield, Chase got an urgent phone call.

"Yes, sir, Mr. Secretary. Will do, sir, 1300 hours."

"Casey, I will have to meet up with you later. I am afraid this cannot wait. I got called in for another job. I am needed in Afghanistan!"

"Can it wait? We need to finish this job."

"Miller has already been informed. I will catch up with you. Good luck!"

"You too, brother."

(Casey thinks out loud, "Well Casey, if you want to know anything about this Chase, you can always go straight to the Secretary. I am always jumping the gun, Chase is a good guy.")

Casey calls Tracy to inform her about digging into Chase's background.

"Hi Tracy, this is Casey."

{"Oh, Casey, do I have news to tell you about your friend Chase…"}

"Tracy, there is a reason why I am calling you. Nevermind about looking into Chase's background."

{"But Casey!!!"}

"I got to go. Catch up with you soon."

As Casey returns to New York, he decides to start digging around to see what the word was out on the streets. He found out that the two Mafia's gangs were bumping heads, one of them was trying to take over the other's territory. A phone call comes in. It is his Boss, Miller.

{"Casey"}

"Yes Sir Mr. Miller."

{"I have sent you two agents to New York. Chase will not be coming back any time soon. Do you need back up?"}

"Yes Sir!"

{"I want some news on what is going on. We need to find those explosives. I cannot tell you how important this is to me and your country Casey."}

Casey needed to get some answers and details on the two gangs that are beefing. One of them must be involved and know the whereabouts of the explosives. Casey heads to Harlem to see if he can find out anything about the case. He pokes around the Barbershop where different low life's, gang members, mafia sources, corrupt cops, crooked lawyers, and corrupt judges go when they need a haircut. People come in and go out of the shop every day. He remembers Beavers Barbershop at the end of Lexington Ave. Casey walks into the barbershop and spots gold ole Joe, the owner.

"Joe, my man. It has been a while."

"What brings you here, Casey?"

"Just thought I would drop in to check on a friend."

"Well Casey, it depends on what kind of friend category I fall beneath. A snitch friend, an undercover snitch friend, snitch friend running for their life, or a lucrative snitch friend. Take your pick. Whatever you came here for, I do not have, want, nor do I need it."

"It is nothing like that. I just thought I would drop in on a good friend."

"Every time you drop in, you either want information or are in some sort of trouble. What is it this time?"

"Word on the streets is that someone brought some explosives from the Russian Mafia. It was also said that the two crime syndicate Mafia leaders here in New York are trying to take over each other's beat. Joe, I know that this is the hot spot for all gossip. I am here because I need your help."

"Help? Man, see what you just did with that word HELP? Just say what you have to say and leave my shop. Mr. Friend, I need my business, and you just ran all my customers out the door. What do you want and make it fast?"

"Joe, can you give me the names of these two leaders?"

"Listen, man, that sounds like Big Ronnie and Blaze, but they call him" Left-hand Blaze."

"See how easy that was. So nice doing business with you Joe."

"Casey, do me a favor; PLEASE do not come back."

Casey walks out, and as he walks up to his car, a man approaches him.

"I heard you've been asking questions?"

"Well... that is none of your concern. Whom may I ask?

"None of your damn business!"

"This business of mine is not complete, but when it is, I will stop."

"YOU WILL STOP NOW!"

The man grabs his shoulder. Casey grabs his hand with a twist and the man screams in pain. Casey pulls the man off him, still holding on to his hand, Casey bent his palm upward and releases him. The man falls to the ground on his knees, holding on to his side. Casey got in his car and makes his way back to his apartment in the upper eastside of Manhattan. Lovely upscale apartment; 2br 2ba. Casey never talks to any of his neighbors. The apartment next door had been empty for two years until he got home to see someone occupying the condo. He walks in his apartment and turns on the lights immediately. Jazz plays in the background as he slowly walks to the refrigerator. His home phone rang. It was Bella.

{"Hello dear, some guy stopped by asking questions about you after you left."}

"Hi, Mother. What kind of question did he ask you?"

{"Oh, just mainly what you do for a living? I told him that you sell cameras to the upper-class businesspeople."}

"What else did he ask you, Mother?"

{"Well, he wondered how long you had been working there."}

"Ma, the next time this man comes over, please call me."

{"Will do son. Talk with you soon. Good night."}

The conversation ends. Casey started thinking that someone stopped by his mother's house showing him two can play this. Someone is hitting close to home. It could be Blaze or Big Ronnie Casey. The phone rings.

"Hello!"

On the other end of the line was a man with a groggy, deep, heavy, whispering voice: {"Stop snooping around where you do not belong or next time you will be without a MOTHER!"}

Click... dial tone. Casey had to start playing it smart. He did not sleep, but meditated that whole night. After his workout studying his martial art moves, he showered and went back to east Harlem. Staying in his car going undercover, he was keeping an eye on Beaver's barbershop. The same man that tried to attack him walks out. Casey needs to make another visit to Joe, but before he makes that visit, he calls his mother.

"Ma, your sister called me and she would like for you to come for a visit to Long Island for a few weeks. Can you do this for me?"

{"Son, you know I do not like going up there; and those cats."}

"Ma, you have not seen your sister in three years."

{"OK, Son, I will only stay for two weeks so please do not ask me to stay any longer."

"Thanks, Ma!"}

Casey's phone rang. It was Miller. This is a busy night, he thought.

"Yes, Sir Mr. Miller."

{"What have you found out so far?"}

"Both Big Ronnie and Left-hand Blaze are fighting over territory, but only one of them have the explosives. Big Ronnie is trying to take over the upper

eastside of Harlem which belongs to Left-hand Blaze. Also, Sir, someone has been snooping around my mother asking questions."

{"Son, seems as though you are ruffing up some feathers?"}

"Yes Sir, it appears as though I am. I need someone keeping a close eye on her. I sent her away for a few weeks, but when she gets back, I need her looked after."

{"Son, I will make that happen."}

"Thank you, Sir."

Things were coming together really fast. He got his mother taken care of so he does not have to worry about her safety. The next morning came very quickly. Casey needs to give Miller a call. He needs to find out more information on these two Mafia bosses Blaze and Big Ronnie. Casey desired a location and details on them. He made a call but got no answer. He might be in a meeting, he thought. He decides to check back later. The phone rings; it is Chase.

{"Hi there Casey."}

"Is everything good in Afghanistan?"

{"The mission is going well. I had to give you a call to let you know that I have some contacts in New York if you need some help on trying to make things right in your backyard. Someone always told me never keep your back yard messy. I regret not being able to back you up."}

"I can surely use this. Thanks for the info. Keep in touch and if you need me call me!"

{"Thanks, brother."}

Chase gave him two names......an arms dealer, who goes by the name of Brandon, and a money launderer named Stella. Brandon is running out of the lower part of Bushwick in Brooklyn and Stella is out of Queens in Jamaica, New York. His first stop was Brandon. Casey checks his gun to make sure he has enough ammunition. Brandon and Stella are running in and out of the dangerous parts of New York, and he was not going to get caught in something he could not get out of. Casey walks up to a steel door and a man was standing outside about the size of Andre' the Giant.

He walked right by as he was trying to figure out how the hell, he was going to get in there without pulling out his gun. He thought briefly about it. Casey walks up to the Giant to ask if he could talk to Brandon. He opened the door; it was that easy. As Casey walks in, he tells Brandon that someone told him he would be able to get some information from him about any activity of any explosives floating around. He asked Brandon if by any chance he would know who is the go-to guy for those explosives. The word on the streets is Blaze is your man, and he was also selling them at a starting price of 2.5 million a pop. That he also has some Russian guy coming in to demonstrate. He did not get any answers, so he decided to leave. As Casey walks out, he starts putting things together. It was getting late, and his phone was ringing. Bella was calling him.

{"Hello, son. How is everything going? Are you eating? You know how you like to miss a few days from eating."}

Casey (half laughing): *"Ma, I am OK. How are aunty and her cats doing?"*

{"You better be glad I made a promise that I am trying to keep or I would be coming home right now."}

"Love you Ma. Talk soon!"

17

As he walked to his car, he got a message on his phone. Miller called while he was in the meeting with Brandon. His message was to let him know that Chase had called him. He told him that he gave Casey some leads that could help him and for him to call for a briefing on the information. The next morning, Casey headed out to Queens for Stella. He came well equipped. He got up in Queens and remembered this place that sold some excellent ole Brazilian food. He stops by Pao De Queijo for some Pao Com Linguica. He loves that Brazilian sausage. Chase gave him Stella's address. It should only be a few blocks from his current position.

He pulls up to Stella's location. It looks like an abandoned building near the water. The windows were armor plated along with steel doors and two men strapped down with weapons and security cameras. He knew he was in the right spot. He thought he would be doing his usual approach. As he walks to the door, one of the men faces him.

"Can I help you?"

Casey (walks up): *"I am here to see Stella."*

"Who are you and what is it you want with Stella?"

"Well, I am a man that is looking for none of your business."

As soon as he went for Casey, Casey jumps up and kicks him in the face. The other guy came at Casey with a gun. Casey leaps up in the air and kicks him in the face with his knee. The weapon falls out of his hand and the man falls to his knees.

"Now let's try this again. I am here to see Stella. Now we could sit out here and play all day long, but I still need to talk with Stella."

Stella (walks out): *"Are you looking for me and who are you?"*

Casey turns towards Stella while straightening his Jacket.

"It's Casey. I need to ask you a few questions."

"Yes!!!"

"Can we take a short walk? Listen I am not going to take up much of your time but I need to know, have you been invited to an auction selling some explosives?"

"Yes, I have. My client needs my business."

"Who is your client?"

"It's Left-Hand Blaze. I am to show up in two days with 8.5 million."

"Do you know where?"

"It is at a warehouse on 257 Seaview Dr. Port Washington."

"Thanks!"

"Do not thank me but Thank Chase because we did him a favor."

Casey could not believe that Chase helped him out tremendously. All that time, he thought that Chase was a trader. He knew someone was snitching and he needed to find out who. He walks to his car and begins driving. As he approaches the warehouse on Seaview Dr., it looks like he was pointed in the right direction. He was wondering how he could get invited to this auction? First things first, he has the whereabouts, next, he needs to get an invitation.

CHAPTER TWO

Snitches Get Stitches

CHASE HELPED HIM out hugely. It is funny how he got assigned to something outside the US like someone did not want him around in this case. It is time for him to start asking how Chase got assigned to a situation outside the US when he was already on a mission. Miller was not in the office but maybe he will be in tomorrow. Casey went home and walked into his apartment. There were lights on next door at an apartment that used to be vacant. As he walked into his apartment, he did his workout and meditated that whole night. The next morning, he made a phone call to Miller.

"Mr. Miller Sir."

"Casey, how is everything going with the case? Chase notified me that he gave you the info about Stella and Brandon and that it should help you out."

"Yes Sir, I got your message. I was calling you to ask how Chase got this assignment when he was already on one?"

"My son, coming from higher up, needed him there more. My boss contacted me. I could have said that we needed him here, but Tracy Fletcher said that she would send two more men agents out. Have they arrived yet?"

"No sir, they have not. It does not look like I will need them. Disregard sending them out here in the field."

"It appears you have everything under control."

"Yes Sir, I do."

"Job well done young man. Carry on then Casey."

"Thank you, Sir."

Casey heads for the warehouse to the new location where the explosives are. As he pulled up at the warehouse, he saw the same man from in front of the barbershop. He knew that this was the right place. Now how can he get in? He does not think he can walk through the front door. He had to walk up some stairs in the rear of the warehouse. As he walked in, he had a front view of everyone looking down at them from upstairs. He sees Brandon, Stella, the man from in front of the barbershop, and two other people. One of them must be Russian and the other one is probably Left-hand Blaze. No explosives are anywhere in sight.

As they talk, Dimitri walks over with a suitcase. It looked like he was about to do a demonstration for the missiles. Casey could not arrest them without the explosives anywhere in sight. They all got in their cars and drove off. He did not think that was going to be the meeting place to demonstrate the explosives. Casey was stuck with a difficult decision. He did not know what was going to happen next. Casey needed to find out what was said in the conversation. His next stop was his old stomping ground, Beavers Barbershop.

It is 0830 hundred hours. Casey sits in front of Beavers Barbershop waiting on Mr. Man. At 0845 hundred hours, Joe opens up the shop and walks Casey.

"Joe, my man, we will meet again."

"Casey, I see you did not get the word which they told you."

"Yes, I met your little friend who got the drop on me from behind. Joe, my man, it seems as though you owe me. It was not right for me to leave and not show you my gratitude for helping me.

"Gratitude, for what?"

"From that ass whipping that I got from your friend that you called on me that day when I stopped by."

Joe (backing up): *"Naw…. Naw Casey. I don't have the law at my feet. I'm out here busting my ass just trying to stay afloat. I do as they ask."*

Casey (picking him up by the shirt): *"You see Joe, I stopped by to thank you."*

Joe was panting and backing up with his hands right out in front of him trying to clear space between him and Casey and to get him to let go of his shirt.

"Naw… Naw… see, I was told that someone was snooping around and for me to give them a call when you get here. I did not know it was you until that day you came in here asking questions."

"Who called you Joe?"

With a long lengthy pause

Joe (panting): *"Um…i..t, um..w a s……It was Blaze man, it was Blaze."*

"Now was that hard my Friend?"

As Casey reels around, Mr. Man walks through the door. Casey turns around intending to say that he was just the man he wants to see. After he pivots, the karate chops him in the throat, walks out the door, and jumps in his car. Someone walks up from behind and gun-butts Casey in the back of the head before he could drive off. As Casey came to, his blindfold came off. He saw a man was sitting in a chair, smoking a cigar.

"We heard you've been giving my people a little bit of trouble."

"...And who may I ask is inquiring?"

"Well, son, my name is Blaze, but people call me left-hand Blaze. I am just wondering why you are asking questions around town, and what do you want?"

"Well, Mr. Blaze, I have been looking into buying some explosives and I heard you are the man."

"Well, you heard wrong."

"I guess I did. You see, my buyer has been looking for some explosives to do a heist job. We are willing to pay top dollar."

"Let's see, maybe I am the right man after all. What do you mean by TOP DOLLAR?"

"It depends on the explosives that you have. We will only pay top dollar. We know good quality when we see it."

"I tell you what, just like I said, maybe I am your man. I just had a shipment come in a few weeks ago from Russia. You and your boss come by. I am having some people come to perform a demonstration. Feel free to bring your money. Stop by and take a look at what I have to offer."

Casey agrees and leaves.

Mr. Man, I need you to find out everything about this Casey person. We do not need any surprises. Call our informer and they will tell you all you need to know about Casey."

Mr. Man makes a phone call but no one picks up.

Meanwhile, Casey gave Miller a call to let him know what took place.

"Sir, I came in contact with Blaze."

{"What... How... did this happen?"}

"Well, see Sir, they took me by surprise."

{"What do you mean TOOK you by surprise?"}

"Well, Sir, I was kind of kidnapped."

{"WHAT! Kidnapped!!....UM, think goodness you made it through.}

(Miller murmured kidnapped)

...wow, now what's next?"

Casey: *"I require money. They invited me to make a bid on the explosives that they have coming in. They have a Russian coming in to do a demonstration. I'm waiting for instructions on the meeting place. Sir, hold on. Someone is at the door."*

As Casey walks to his door, someone slips a letter under the door telling him the meeting place and time.

The meeting place is in upper 'The Bronx'.

"Sir, looks like I received the meeting place."

{"Where will it take place?".}

"The Bronx."

{"Bronx? Casey, I have a funny feeling. That is Big Ronnie's territory. It looks like Blaze is getting a little too bold with this. Casey, be careful. Looks like this is going down tomorrow."}

Casey: *"Do you know when Chase will be coming in because I can sure use his help?"*

{"I wish I could tell you. I haven't a clue, nor have I heard from him other than him notifying me about the two informers he gave you. Casey keep me posted!"}

"Copy that Sir. By the way, Sir, can you tell Tracy Fletcher to give me a call?"

{I will let her know as soon as she gets back from vacation. She was supposed to be gone for two weeks, but she has taken a month off. She's gone to Amsterdam & Budapest for her vacation. She says you only live once."}

Casey finds it very peculiar for her to be on vacation at a time like this. As time gets nearer, Casey finds his way home getting ready for the demo. He sits home and meditates over everything that is going on. As he prepares to turn in, someone knocks at his door. He looks through the aperture and sees a gorgeous woman standing outside his door.

"Hello, Neighbor. I just moved in next to you. My name is Val. Do you have a cup of sugar. Unfortunately, I have not been out shopping yet."

As she walks in, she looks around Casey's apartment. She plants a bug in his room under the stained-brown end table. She will be able to hear what is going on. She wanted to know every conversation that took place inside the apartment and over the phone. He would never know what was going on and she would have intel to what his operations were.

"I did not give you, my name."

"Well, are you planning on telling me your name?"

"Yeah, you can call me Rush or Roulette."

"Oh OK, I think I will call you Roulette."

"Whatever you want!"

"Well, I just stopped by to introduce myself and to get some sugar. I am happy you had some."

"I'm glad I did too, good night!"

As he closes the door behind her, he does not know that she planted the bug in his room. He turns in for the night. The next morning comes, and as he awakes, he has a note stuck under his door. The note specified the place and the time for the demonstration:

New Jersey, Franklin Lakes on Nature Preserve Way owned by Left Hand Blaze.

Casey gives Miller a call, but he is not in his office. He leaves a message on his answering machine letting him know where the location is. While getting everything ready for the demonstration, someone knocks on his door. As he opens the door, it is his next-door neighbor.

Mr. Roulette, I am sorry for asking you, but I need another cup of sugar."

"Lady look, there is a store around the corner. I need to get ready."

"Why are you in such a rush Roulette?"

"I just got a sale on some of my camera's. It's a big sale so I need to meet these people before I lose my contract. Have a good day!"

As he shuts the door behind her, she starts talking to someone through her ear.

"Tell the guys it looks like something is going down today. Keep your ears and your eyes open. Follow him; DO NOT LOSE HIM!!!!"

As she walks into her apartment, she hears Casey's door shut. She let the guys know that he just left his apartment. She phones her boss to let him know that Casey is on the move.

Casey reaches New Jersey for the showcase. He meets up with the rest of the gang. Another vehicle pulls up, but it is far off. It is Val and three other people inside a black van. Dimitri pulls up, Blaze, Stella, then Brandon follows immediately after. As Dimitri pulls his tools out for the Demonstration, his head henchmen come up towards him and whispers in his ear.

"It looks like we must postpone this sorry for your inconvenience."

When he was getting ready to leave, a van, ten unmarked cars, and a helicopter covered all over the area coming in full force.

Val (screaming): *"STOP NSA!"*

Dimitri's car pulls up; both Dimitri and Blaze get in and make a clean getaway. Val was looking straight at Casey, and she tells him to do exactly what she says, and his cover will not get blown. He complies. She pulls him to the ground like a dirty Drug dealer and handcuffs him. They are all taken to the NSA government building. Val walks into the room where they had Casey.

"Well, Mr. Roulette."

"Cut the crap. You know who I am. Why am I here?"

27

Miller (makes an appearance on the scene): *"Because I told her to bring you here."*

"What is this and why am I here?"

"We could not blow your cover, so this was the only way. We have some bad news…we have a mole."

"Mole, what do you mean?"

"We had some agents to go in and get Chase where he was camped. Looks like the camp he was located at had been ransacked. We are searching for him and his field agents and still no luck. No one knew he was out there but the agency. I thought that you needed to know this. I will not lose any more of my agents. I asked for help from a friend of mine that runs NSA. Could I borrow some of the best field agents he had. I see you met Val…"

"Shh yes, I did. Sir, you had her move in next door to me?"

"Just keeping you safe by watching your back. I also thought you needed help. Knowing that Chase is on another assignment, I figured you needed someone to have your back right now."

"I understand Sir. Next time, could you give me a little warning, please? Sir, any word from Tracy Fletcher?"

"Nope, not a peep Casey, why you ask?"

"I don't know how to put it. I don't know if I want to put it out there. I think your mole is Tracy Fletcher!"

"Come on, Casey, do you have proof or just bits and pieces nothing concrete? I think it goes beyond our reach, including yours."

"Well, when I get that proof, then we will talk."

Meanwhile, looking at the camp, Chase began thinking that

something was off. Chase had gone deep into the woods to bring back food. As he walked around his perimeter, it had nearly been burned to the ground. He was walking around stunned, puzzled, and thinking who could have done such a thing. One of the men came out of hiding telling him that they were there looking for him. He had to make sure he understood what the man was saying to him and wondered why him? The man replied that he heard them talking, telling each other that they cannot let Chase get back to the US. He let Chase know that they never said why. The man went looking for Chase, but as they headed his way, he hid until they left.

Chase takes his men to a safe place. He was trying to get his thoughts together. He was confused and the first thing that came to mind was letting them know back home what took place and that he was okay. The intercoms were down at his camp. He had a two-day walk ahead to the nearest camp that had mainland phones. As he walked through the woods, trying not to get noticed, he heard men's voices. These men were on a portable phone talking to a voice he recognized but could not place it right then. Her voice sounded settled and soft-spoken. After they got off the phone, Chase had an idea. He needed that phone to call back home. He was about two miles ahead of them, so he climbs a tree and falls on top of two men and knocks them out cold. The other one pulls out a long knife tossing it from left to right telling Chase he was going to gut him from his navel to his throat. The man charges straight at Chase. Chase did a sidekick to the throat, the man got back up. Chase then grabs his arm and twists it to his back. In the process, he grabs his neck and shifts it from left to right causing the man to fall like a pile of bricks. Chase walks a couple of steps and people start coming outside as he walks inside the camp.

Chase (asks the lady in her language-Pashto): *"Can I use your phone?"*

She walks back to her home, and he follows her. The phone rings at Langley. The operator picks up.

{"Camera hall shop, how may I help you?"}

"This is field agent Chase. I need Miller."

{"Hold please!"}

Putting Chase on hold, Miller was reached in the Field.

{"Miller speaking!"}

"Sir; this is Chase!"

{"Chase! What is going on? Are you okay? What happened?"}

"I am not sure, but someone does not want me back home. What is going on, Sir?"

{"Son, it is a whole heap of a mess here. You need a lift son."}

"Yes, Sir, I thought you would never ask."

{"I will send out a plane at 0200 hours. Have your men ready and waiting.}

Hangs up and begins talking to Casey.

"Casey, good news...that was Chase."

"How is Chase?"

"Well, he is in good spirits. I do not know the details, but he is on his way to Langley to get briefed."

"Keep me posted Sir?"

"Will do son. I need you to play nice with Val."

"Me, I am always lovely. They call me Mr. Nice guy."

Val walks in.

"Can you tell me what you have learned about these explosives??"

"Not much since you came and bulldozed your way in. Now we both do not know a thing."

"Can you keep the NSA posted as well?

CASEY!"

Casey (stands up): *"YEAH!"*

"Your bail has been posted; you are free to go."

Detective Riley gave him back his things and told him to stay clean. As Casey walks out the door, Left-Hand Blaze pulls up in his town car telling Casey to get in.

"I appreciate you posting my bail."

"Well, we are business partners."

"Mr. Blaze, not just yet. We still have some unfinished business to do. Get in touch with me when you're ready."

The driver stops the car and Casey gets out. Just as he walks away, a van with tinted windows pulls up. It's Val and her crew.

"Casey got in. Was that Left-Hand Blaze that just dropped you off?"

Casey: *"He is snooping, and you need to lay low Val."*

"Did he say something to make you think he was snooping?"

"Nope, just a hunch. Lay low Val and I will call you."

Casey is ready to be in for the night. As he walks up towards his front door, he spots a white piece of paper sticking out telling him to be ready at 0500 hundred hours. Casey gave Miller a call letting him know what was going down. Miller told Casey to let him know the location as soon as he gets it. The next morning at 0500 hundred hours, Casey stands outside his apartment waiting on Blaze. As he spots a black Escalade with tinted windows pull up and he gets in. Left hand Blaze had a car sent to pick him up but Blaze was nowhere in sight. They pull up at his home. There was a crowd of vehicles there. Stella and Brandon both pull up at the same time. Blaze home is set on 2000 acres of land overlooking the Hudson River. The George Washington Bridge could be seen from the right of his home. Casey was impressed. He walked up and knocked on the door. They were all greeted by a butler. They could tell it was a busy morning walking through the kitchen seeing the waiters, waitresses, and cooks. Casey saw one of the cooks that looked familiar. He thought about it, but he could not recollect right then. As they continued through the kitchen out into the backyard, they were all greeted by Blaze himself.

"Blaze, what a charming home you have."

"Yes, business has been good to me and my family. We are sitting on 2000 acres of land that was passed down from generation to generation and I brought more land on top of that... Since everyone is here, we can begin."

Dimitri walks out with a black suitcase. He was showing everyone the duds to the demonstration before he began. It is a computerized explosive that Dimitri set to detonate 200 acres out. He sent a notification to the dud's explosives. The explosive blasted at the set acres out. They all hopped in the jeep and rode out to the area. The missile left a hole the size of the Grand Canyon. After the demonstration, the bid started at 3.5 million dollars. Iran bid 10 million dollars and the first bid ends with the bid from Iran. Casey knew he could not move in on what was going on because the real explosives were nowhere in sight. He had to call Langley, so he stepped away from everyone to call Mr. Miller.

"Sir, they are selling explosives as we speak. Blaze sold the first one to Iran (country). He is selling one per day. The next demonstration is not until tomorrow. We have plenty of time to try and figure out what's our next move. Sir, can you fill Val in on what is going on?"

{"Will do, keep me posted."}

"Have you heard from Tracy Fletcher?"

{"Not yet, but I will keep you posted. Her vacation ends in another week."}

"Sir, I noticed one of the cooks that was at the Blaze mansion but I could not place where I knew him from. If I get a picture of that cook, would you run it through the system?

{"As soon as we get the picture, I will run it through our database."}

Casey walks through his door and spots a note left on the floor.

Be there at 0200 hundred hours and don't be late.

Meanwhile, Miller gets a phone call from Chase telling him that there was something he had to get off his chest.

"Chase, is there something you are not telling me?"

{"Sir, I was trying not to say, but I think you have a mole in your company."}

"What is up with you and Casey?"

{"What does Casey have to do with this?"}

"Well Casey is thinking the same thing. He seems to believe it is Tracy Fletcher. I am going to investigate this myself. Chase, keep this between you and me. Casey doesn't need to know about this. Did they say how long you are going to be in Briefing?"

{"NO SIR. They are telling me it could take a few weeks because of what took place. They are trying to find out who is trying to contain me."}

Meanwhile, Casey is trying to get things going because he has only one more day to get those explosives. He is walking out the door giving himself time to get there. He drives up in the driveway in 1930 hundred hours giving him time to look around before the auction starts. He snoops around Blaze home outside his shed. He pulls out his tools to pick up the lock. He slowly walks inside just as two guards pass by with guns bulging outside their lean tight bodies. He starts snooping and sees three big crates with Russian writing on them. The crates were there but the explosives were not. He starts snooping even more. As he walks around, the door swings open. Cook thought he remembered but could not place. He is snooping around as well but why, who is he? Casey hides behind some boxes looking at the cook wondering why he is searching for the room. More people start coming around that area as the auction is about to begin. The cook sneaks out and heads back to the kitchen. Casey carefully walks out getting caught up by Val.

"Val, what the hell are you doing?"

"Casey, I'm trying to find out what you're doing. I gave you a secure job to keep me posted. What do you have?"

"Let the boss know that the explosives are here from what I can tell but I still have not located them. I was only able to find the crates they came in.

No need to go in full blast because they might not be here. He has already sold one and is waiting to sell the rest of them and ship them all out at once."

"Copy that. I will let Miller know what is going on."

Dimitri comes walking out with Blaze and this time Big Ronnie is there. Blaze and Big Ronnie greet each other. Blaze let Ronnie know that he is not welcome there and insisted that he leave. Blaze men escorted him off the property. Everyone is whispering and gawking as Big Ronnie walks out. He made eye contact with the cook. The Cook then nodded back at Big Ronnie. It was only then that Casey remembered who the cook was. He belonged to Big Ronnie's gang, and he is relaying information back to Big Ronnie. That is how he knew about the auction.

Blaze spoke to his men, and they walked out. Dimitri is preparing for his dud Demonstration. This time they had the Iraqis to join them securely online. They are trying to get in on the action as well. Dimitri set the explosives 350 miles out. The night of the auction they both set up the conference call for invitation only. As Blaze turns facing Dimitri, he starts sending in the coordinates on how far he was launching the dud explosives out. The missile begins to ignite and a burst of fiery flames roar throughout the midnight sky. It launched out over Blaze estate rapidly speeding over the George Washington Bridge like a meteor crossing over the air. The fiery flames lit up the dark atmosphere of New York moving towards the Montauk Lighthouse. The passing missile caused the lighthouse to shake like an airplane going through turbulence, causing it to shatter the windows to pieces. It pierced through the Atlantic Ocean and shook the bottom layer of the ocean floor. The demonstration was a success. Everyone was on their phones with their Bosses letting them know that the demonstration is a positive investment.

The bid started with 10.5 million from Iraq.

The next bid came in from South Korea at 11.5 million.

The next one is 12.5 million from North Korea.

The last bid came in with 15 million from Japan... SOLD.

Blaze walks off giving Japan the details and bank numbers for the deposit.

"Ladies and Gents, that is it for tonight. Tomorrow is our last show. Details will be sent to you an hour before the event. If you are late the door will be locked, you will not be able to bid. Have a good evening."

Blaze walks off. Casey must get back into the shed. He sent the picture off for Miller to investigate the cook identification, because even though he portrays himself as one thing, he still needed more intel on him. Val is sitting in Casey's back seat waiting for him. He gets inside his car. Val pops up from the back seat with papers that Miller gave her.

"WHAT! The hell... (pausing)... you're going to give me an aneurysm."

Val places the documents in Casey's hand. He was right. He already suspected the cook's name was Walter and he was only pretending to work in the kitchen for Blaze, but he really works for Big Ronnie, and he is spying on Blaze and feeding Big Ronnie information.

"What is he up to Casey? What is going on and why are you so curious about this cook?"

Casey intends to find out why Big Ronnie is spying on Blaze.

"Val, I need a favor...can you go back and see if Walter has any family? If my hunch is right, we have a bigger problem. Val do me this favor, please!"

"I will get back to you with the information, but after that, I want some answers."

Val walks off to her van, they drive off, and she immediately gets on the phone with the NSA. Val tells her boss what has been going down with the explosives and the auctioning off the missiles. She then asks her boss if he can investigate a cook that is working for Left Hand Blaze who goes by the name Walter. She figured he must have a record being with that type of crowd.

"Val, you are not giving me much to work with. Give me a few hours and I will get back with you."

Meanwhile, Casey walks into his apartment. He gets a phone call from Miller letting him know that Tracy Fletcher asked for another week off. They granted it to her. Miller told Casey that if he is right about Tracy Fletcher, he wants it solved before she gets back off her vacation. After his phone call from Miller, he starts his meditation along with doing his martial arts workout. He hears a knock on his door; it's Val. He invites her in. She pushes the papers on his chest.

"What is going on? You cannot keep me in the dark."

As he reads the paper, Val is still talking in his ear.

Casey (turns around): *"Has anyone ever told you they are annoying?"*

"Well Mr. Rush Roulette, has anyone ever told you...."

Before she could finish her sentence, a piece of paper slid under his door.

Tomorrow at 2100 hundred hours do not be late.

"Casey, why did you need more data on this Walter?"

As he reads, he sees that Tracy Fletcher is the sibling of Walter.

"I was dead on. This changes everything. (turns around facing Val)

One of Blaze's cooks' sisters works for the CIA!"

"WHO!?"

"The cook I caught snooping around the shed when you walked up when I was coming out of the shed that day."

"Do you believe that Tracy Fletcher has been feeding information back to her brother?"

"YES! That is how they knew we were coming that day in Russia and that is how they got Chase reassigned. Also, that's how Big Ronnie walked into the auction."

"But what does Big Ronnie have to do with this? What are we going to do?"

"That I do not know, but we need to find out why Walter is spying on Blaze."

"Well, from what I see, that is your snitch right there. We need to find out what is her motive for working at the CIA and why is Walter working for Blaze!"

Casey calls Miller to let him know what he found out. He picks up the phone.

{*"Casey, you have something for me?"*}

"Sir, I think you need to set down for this."

As he tells Mr. Miller his new found information, Mr. Miller falls back in his seat. Miller was highly disappointed. All this time he did not know that she was the traitor.

{"I didn't even know she had a brother working for the Mafia. So Casey, she's been feeding information to her brother this whole time?"}

"It seems that way Boss."

{"Ok. Now we have proof, so we must be smart about this."}

"Yes Sir, copy that. So, what is next? Sir, I was thinking maybe we can play along a little bit longer."

{"We need to block her security clearance. Copy that, Casey."}

"No Sir. Then she will know something is up. We play along, but we keep tabs on her clearance and monitor her being on the computer."

{"I will have the guys watch her movements. We got to be quick about this Casey because there is no telling how far this thing goes or how much Tracy Fletcher knows."}

The next day was the beginning of the week. Tracy Fletcher comes in regular as usual. She does her daily activities and brings coffee in for Miller.

"Ah good morning, Tracy Fletcher. How was your trip?"

Sir, it was beautiful. I got to relax, and I got a lot done. My hair, my nails; I feel like a brand-new woman. Did I miss anything?

"Nope, not really. Oh yes, Chase is back."

Tracy Fletcher (looks puzzled): *"Oh, really?"*

"Is something the matter Tracy?"

"No Mr. Miller."

Tracy then walks to the restroom to call Walter. He picks up the phone. She tells Walter that Chase is back in the country.

{"What…why…how, never mind. My work here is almost done. I need you to find out what all the CIA knows about the explosives."}

"NSA…Walter you need to get out of there. Oh yeah, you did not know the NSA is in on this as well.

{"Dammit! You don't think I've tried. Big Ronnie wants the info on the last auction. He is working to set up shops on all the lower east side of Harlem. After he heard about Blaze and some explosives, he wanted to get in on the action, but Blaze kicked him out before he even had a chance. That is why he is trying to get all the lower east side of Harlem. Tracy and Blaze is too busy even to notice what Big Ronnie is doing. He is trying to clean him out big time. He offered me a promotion that is a significant pay increase if I help him out. With that money, we can start our own business."}

"Walter!"

{"Tracy, you trust me, right? Let me do this."}

Tracy starts snooping around the office. Miller came out to ask her to get Chase on the phone please. Tracy tries to call Chase but no answer.

"Mr. Miller, I did not get a response."

"He might still be in the Briefing. Someone was trying to keep him from coming back home. We need to brief you on what has been going on around here, but it will have to wait. The auction is going on tonight."

"Auction? What are you talking about…what auction?

Miller just walks off. Tracy starts thinking hard. She was wondering if Walter knows the auction is tonight. She tries to give Walter a call but he is not picking up. Walter is back snooping around the estate of Blaze mansion. He has been walking for almost an hour before he notices that there is another shed about 25 miles from the villa. As he walks around the hut, he sees Dimitri messing around with something. He is packing the explosive getting them ready to ship out. As Walter starts backing up, someone came up from behind him and hit him over the head with a brick. Walter falls to the ground. One of Dimitri's men brought him in the shed, bounded, and gagged Walter. They load the explosives into the truck and move them on the other side. They left Walter inside the shed and began heading back for the auction starting at 2100 hundred hours.

It is now 1900 hundred hours. Tracy is still trying to contact her brother Walter with no luck. She takes matters into her own hands and tries to contact Big Ronnie, but no answer. Tracy knew something was wrong, but who could she trust. She knew they were all doing wrong, but most of all, she did not want to get arrested and go to prison for treason. The only thing there was for her to do was leave. She and Walter talked about if this day had ever come, she was to pack up her things and go back to where they call home. The whole vacation was for her to set up everything for her and Walter only in case that day ever came. She left the office with no warning. She stopped by Walter's home where he buried half a million dollars for emergencies. She had never unpacked from her vacation from when she left the airport. She called Walter again, but still no answer. She did not stop until she got to the airport.

The last call for flight 2600 to Budapest came out over the loudspeaker.

She boards the plane at 2100 hundred hours, the same precise time as the auction.

In the meantime, things were going well back at Blaze's mansion. Casey brought along Miller introducing him as the one wanting to buy the explosives. They brought 20 million with them in a case and they had Val accounting for Miller with his money. Dimitri walks outside with his dud demonstration and Blaze is right behind him preparing to set up. This time they had China and Bulgaria online along with other countries right there in Blaze backyard. Dimitri opens fire 550 acres out. He hit something and it exploded; damn near shook half New York to where some pieces of debris from George Washington Bridge fell in Hudson River. The Traffic on Washington Bridge came to a STOP! Everyone at the auction jumps into their jeeps and sped down to the spot where the shed once stood. Dimitri did this; the fire was so bad they called in for the fire department.

"Blaze, are they going to do an investigation because we had left someone in there?"

Blaze (looking at Dimitri in disbelief): *"WHAT!"*

"Yeah man, it was your cook. He had been snooping around the shed. We had to move the explosives on the other end, and we left him bound there."

They turn the sprinklers on outside to make sure the fire does not spread.

The bid started at 12.5 million.

China bid 15.5 million

Bulgaria Bid 18.5 million

Miller Bid 19 million

Bulgaria came back and bid 19.5 million.

Miller came in to offer 20 million, but before Blaze could say SOLD

China came in with 20.5 million SOL...before he could say SOLD to China this voice came in clear across the crowd

25.5 million.

Everyone looks back to see who that voice belongs to. What was an Asian man doing there? Is he bidding for China? Everyone is puzzled about who he is and who hired him. Blaze did not care because he made 25.5 million in one night.

"Sir, we have an account number that you can transfer your money to."

"NO need. I have CASH!"

Blaze eyes were bulging from his socket.

"Did he say CASH?"

Blaze notified everyone the AUCTION IS OFFICIALLY CLOSE!

All eyes are on this man who had bid for his Boss. Everyone wants to know who his boss is. They did not stare at him casually but were wondering, with disbelief, about who would have so much money 'in cash'.

Blaze (with skepticism): *"Sir, I need your bank information."*

Asian Man: *"Again, no need. I brought CASH!"*

Blaze mouth falls to the ground. The man notifies his boss that he won the bid. Who the hell would have that much cash on them? Big Ronnie walks in, greets Blaze, and gives Blaze his address for his explosives that he had just bought.

"You have a very beautiful place here. You know business has been good for me as well since I took over Harlem's lower and upper east side. Oh, by the way, the guys at Beavers Barbershop say hello, such nice guys. I told them I have taken over that area and that they now answer me. We both are into making money."

Left-hand Blaze (too upset to even thank his company for coming): *"Someone tell me why you all have not been out there in the streets making sure our assets were good to go? Big Ronnie has taken over my territory. It is not going to be easy to get it back."*

Blaze (marching up to Big Ronnie): *"Your shipment will be there tomorrow evening."*

Blaze stays up that whole night getting the guys together.

"Everyone, work your way to that shed and dispose of that body somewhere in the woods."

A little later, Casey and Miller worry about how they are going to get those explosives.

"Sir, I know that they are on his property. We can get a search warrant."

"We would be taking a big risk by guessing that they are on his property."

"Any suggestions Val?"

"YES, I DO! Wait till late and just take them back? They don't belong to him. The government wants it back, so we take it back. Casey, does that sound like a plan?"

"Val, I like the way you think. YES SIR, that is a plan."

"Then we all meet back up here at 0100 hours. When we get there, you will have an hour at 0200 hours. There will be a pickup at the same drop off spot. Then this mission will be complete.

Blaze men formed together and drove far off and buried the body deep in the woods. Casey and Val assemble a team to go undercover to take back the explosives and announce to everyone to be safe. The Sikorsky UH-60 Black Hawk picked up the agents and the drop were delivered safely. They came up from the back of the mansion and covered all the sheds Blaze had on his grounds.

"Casey, are you sure about the crates being at that location?"

"Yes, I am sure they were here."

"Do you think he could have already shipped them?"

"No way! He could not have sent them out that fast."

"Time to go."

They heard the Black Hawk riding in midair. They all headed back to the drop off point. The pilot gave Casey the phone. It was Miller. Casey took the call.

"Sir, we did not find the explosives. They are not there."

{"I know. Chase called and told us they got a tip. Dimitri stole them back from Blaze and he has a private jet waiting at the airfield. The pilot is taking you all there now."}

"Yes Sir!"

Casey told Val what was taking place.

"How did Dimitri get those weapons out from under Blaze?"

Casey: *"I do not know, but we need to hurry up and get to the airfield."*

As they approached the airstrip, the plane was sitting there. Dimitri walks back to the flight, but he spots the CIA & NSA coming, so he ran to the aircraft as they were pulling up. The plane starts descending as they pull up trying to stop the aircraft. Casey deviates in front, slowing down and swerving. The jet tries to accelerate.

"Val, take the steering wheel."

"WHY!"

"Just take it!"

Casey jumps up, with his jacket in his hand, and stands up in the seat.

"Val, slow down so I can jump on the landing gear."

"What?"

She looks at him and the car swerves, but she regains control of it. She slows down so Casey can jump on the landing gear. The plane rises at an incline. The front landing gear is getting ready to close so Casey stuffs his jacket in the landing gear stopping the wheel from closing. The plane drops altitude. The aircraft was so low until people on the ground could be seen looking up at the plane. Dimitri comes out of the cockpit to the cargo compartment near the landing gear trying to get rid of Casey. He grabs Dimitri's hand; forcing him off the plane. Dimitri loses his grip and tumbles off the plane onto the ground with Casey following right behind. Dimitri was banged up pretty bad with blood flowing down his face from a dash across his eyebrow. Val rush to their sides as Dimitri gets up and tries to make a run for it, but Casey runs behind him. He catches up to Dimitri and delivers a blow to the back of his head. Dimitri falls down and they both start doing hand to hand combat. Dimitri was getting the best of Casey. When Casey turns around, Dimitri kicks him in the face. Casey goes down, but as he gets back up, he sweeps his leg right from under Dimitri. As they both begin hand to hand combat again, Casey did a Krav Maga move by blocking his punch. Dimitri goes down and jumps right back up, but before he could get in another position, Casey comes back with a side kick to Dimitri's head. He goes down and Casey grabs Dimitri and turns him around. Val runs over and Casey cuffs Dimitri. The agents come to put Dimitri in the van.

"Yeah Val, I am fine."

"Do we need to pick up Blaze as well?"

"We can only get him for selling illegal weapons. We got Dimitri with the explosives. That will put him away for a while."

"What about Big Ronnie?"

"We can only get him for buying stolen goods that he never got. What we need to find out is how far Red Dawn goes. We know back to Russia, but how much of a distance in Russia? Dimitri did not seem like the head man in charge. We need to investigate him. Call Miller and let him know we are bringing in Dimitri."

They pull up to Langley. Miller walks up to Casey to let him know that Tracy Fletcher has disappeared.

"Can you track her?"

"We got as far as Amsterdam and then the trace went cold."

"Why did she run?" Do you know?"

"I was trying to figure that out. Maybe she felt we was closing in on her."

"Can't be because we never gave her a reason that we were on to her. Something else must have happened. Where is her brother Walter?"

47

"We do not know. He seems to have disappeared as well."

Chase walked up to Casey, congratulating him on a job well done.

"We heard you went for a plane ride in mid-air."

"Yeah, but we got him."

"That is for damn sure. So now what Casey?'

Miller walks in with a well-dressed man wearing handmade Italian shoes.

"Who is that, Casey?"

"Don't know."

After Miller walks the gentleman to the back, he steps up to Casey letting him know that the gentleman is Dimitri's lawyer.

They all replied LAWYER and agreed that the move was fast.

"Yes, he came out of nowhere."

Blaze (barges in): *"I demand to speak with Dimitri!"*

"NO VISITORS because he is in interrogation."

"Then I will wait until I am sure he is put away!" (pacing the floor until Dimitri was locked up in his cell).

Val (talking to Casey and Miller): *"Blaze is feeling it right now. All that money he has collected and now he has nothing to give those people. Why would he care? He is the damn Mafia. Blaze can go anywhere in the world. He has plenty of dough."*

"Where can he go?

"Yes, you're right. Still, it just does not add up."

The Lawyer walks off to give Dimitri Dad a call.

{"Can you get my son out of jail?"}

Lawyer: *"Sorry sir, your son is into something bigger than you and I?"*

{"Did you find out what he was doing?"}

"Well, he brought some explosives from Alek and that's not all. It seems that your son and Alek were trying to run a con on one of the local Mafia families."

{"That kolot' (prick in English). Give me a name. What kind of con?"}

"The Blaze Family. They call him Left-hand Blaze. Dimitri took the explosives back from Blaze after he killed his cook."

{"WHAT?"}

"The cook goes by the name Walter. He started snooping around Blaze estate and saw Dimitri inside one of the sheds. Dmitri was moving the explosives for one point to the other. Walter got caught, Dimitri tied him up and left him in the shed. Dimitri did a real demonstration from one of his explosives, instead of doing a dud demonstration, that he kept for himself and he blew up the hut and killed Walter. After, Blaze and his men went and buried the body. Your son took all the explosives back. Alek was a 'jack of all trades. He was a computer Wizkid; setting up fraudulent Swiss accounts and handling the money."

{"...and what else?"}

"Whenever money was being put into Blaze's account, Alek linked his computer up with Blaze's computer through team viewer and took those funds putting the money into another account. Blaze was selling the explosives via auction online purchase. Sir, your son, is in a heap of a

mess, and there is no way he will be getting out anytime soon. I also ran into Blaze. He wanted to talk with your son."

{"Who is this Casey I keep hearing about?"}

"Mr. Petrov, that is the CIA agent that arrested your son?"

{"Wait for my further instructions."}

Blaze heads back home very pissed and wondering how this could have happened. He started making plans on how to pay back the money they took from him. He sold some of his assets to cover what they had received from those people—letting them know that he also had been vandalized by trusting Dimitri. He told all the buyers that Dimitri had their money, but he was willing to pay them back. Blaze needed to make an example of Dimitri for what he did. He hired some inmates to kill Dimitri for taking what was rightfully his. His next man in charge asks him if he thinks that is wise.

"This man came into my home, killed my cook, and took back the explosives that I brought from him so why are you asking me such a thing? I WANT HIM KILLED!!!"

CHAPTER THREE
Doomsday

"DIMITRI HAS TAKEN so much from me. I have lost millions of dollars, so he doesn't deserve to live another day. I need that handled."

"Do you know who Dimitri's father was?"

Ron, his right-hand man, tried to explain the situation.

"To be honest, I do not think you really want to get yourself involved in that. His father was a hitman for the mafia back in Russia and his father's boss left him his fortune before he passed away. He is known all over the crime syndicate families. You do not want to get yourself strung up like this."

"I thank you for telling me all this, but I still need Dimitri gone... demolished."

"Sir, he is more powerful than you will ever imagine."

"Well Ron, again I thank you for telling me this. It does not change how I feel though so don't make me tell you this again. I need that bastard gone before the end of the day. Can you get in contact with our little friend 'the paper pusher'.... What's her name?"

"Well, sir, that is another problem she is nowhere in sight."

Scott V.L. Mack

"What do you mean?"

"How can I put it…. she left without a trace."

Blaze (baffled): *"Do you mean to tell me the little miss nobody just disappeared without a trace? Find her. Find her today!"*

Ron is sweating bullets. On his second day being Blaze's right-hand man, he is making phone call after phone call tracing her number and he is still coming up with dead-ends. Her last whereabouts was Amsterdam. Tracy Fletcher is a brilliant woman. She must have ditched her phone after Amsterdam. There is no way she can be traced. Ron walks back in and explains to blaze about Tracy Fletcher's last whereabouts.

Back at Langley, Miller, Casey, and Val were all on a conference call with the Secretary of State. After they notify the Secretary to keep him in the loop, he requires them to do whatever it takes to find out if there is another person involved. Casey starts making phone calls back to the motherland, Russia. His phone calls confirm that it was only Dimitri and Alek, but on that phone call, he also finds out who Dimitri's father is. He ran a trace on Dimitri father and found out that he is big-time Mafia back in Russia. Casey also found out that he became a big-time Mafia after his boss died and left him his empire. He is well-liked around the syndicate families.

"Bad news, how the hell does a well-off young man get himself involved in a shitty ass scam? He has made an enemy here in the US. Blaze already has a sneaky way of getting things done, but he is going to have more than just Blaze after him. Those people have invested in something that he has taken from them. Blaze raised enough money to pay them back. Dimitri has made a hell of a lot more people angry, and in the process, made many enemies. I don't think Blaze is going to let this go. Boss, I think we need to

keep a close eye on Dimitri. Something is telling me that this is far from being over. We are going to need extra agents when we move him to court."

Miller: "Well guys, job well done. Why don't you and Val go and get some rest and be back here at 0800 hundred hours."

Casey: "Yes Sir!"

Casey and Val walk out of the building and they spot the lawyer going back in. Casey's mind has him thinking that Dimitri's lawyer is up to something. Not much he can do because Dimitri is going to jail for an exceptionally long time. The next morning, Casey came in early at 0700 hundred hours. When he walks in, he notices that Miller never left; he was there the entire night. Something had to be wrong. Casey walks in his office. The conference call just ends with the Secretary of State.

Miller (looking up at Casey): "Sit down!"

Casey (sits down immediately): "What is wrong?"

"I have some lousy news... Dimitri is walking out."

"WHAT?"

"Calm down Casey. Dimitri has diplomatic immunity."

"Sir, I do not understand. I cannot believe this. All of this was for nothing. He can just waltz into the US and do as he damn pleases. It is not possible. What kind of clout does he have? He is walking out just as we are in discussion."

"It is his father. He made a few phone calls."

Val (walks in): "Have I missed something?"

"Alot Val. We were just told that Dimitri has Diplomatic Immunity."

53

"Wait...this is not bad. We can actually play with this."

"Explain yourself, Val."

"Maybe Blaze will try to off him once he gets out and Dimitri will have to come running back for help. Sir, when is he getting out on bail?

"He is getting out as we speak. His lawyer is posting his bail."

Casey (walks in to talk with his lawyer): *"Please let Dimitri know that if he ever needs our help, we are just a phone call away."*

That's not necessary. We have everything under control. Come along Dimitri, your father is waiting back at home."

(walks by Casey with a little smirk, whispering softly): *"If you are ever in Russia, please look me up. I will give you a Grand Tour; Russian style."*

Casey (walking up to him aggressively): *"Is that a threat?"*

"No, just being me...Dasvidaniya!" (goodbye in Russian).

As he walks out, Val is standing in his view. He winks at her. As she looked at him; she was disgusted. She turns around to Miller.

"I would like to slice that smirk off his face."

"Val, I did not know you had it in you."

"Sir, you haven't seen anything yet."

"Maybe your boss has been keeping you in the office far too long."

"Maybe, maybe not. Sir, there is a reason why he keeps me in the office. Two years ago, I was the lead agent on a case. Big Ronnie and the Boston Mafia son were involved. We got caught up in a crossfire, and his son died from my gun shot. They arrested me, and when I went to trial, I was found innocent. He pulled his gun out and he was pointing it at a young

pregnant female. She leaned over from him just in time. I was able to take a clean shot and I watched him crumble to the ground. With so much blood, I knew he was gone before he touched the ground. His men came in and confiscated his gun to make it look like I just killed an innocent man that was not armed. They tried to frame me. The only thing that saved me was the fact the restaurant had a video that was viewed by the internal investigation officers."

"Wow, I did not know that!"

"That's not all. It appears that Big Ronnie has a soft heart. He brought the video into court, presented it to my lawyer, and I was acquitted. I decided to take some time off from being a field agent. My boss asked me if I was ready to get back out there. He had a small case; nothing major, so here I am. Sir, can you excuse me please?"

"Yes, of course."

Val's cell was vibrating in her skirt pocket. When she answered, her boss asked her to come in. She told Miller that she would be back later. Miller told Val to take the rest of the day off and that they will call her if anything changes. Val walks out the door behind Dimitri and his lawyer. A car pulls up at a fast pace and throws a black round ball out the window. As soon as the ball touches the ground, it explodes with a loud BOOM! The boom had gone off with a loud noise and the explosion was so powerful it shook the whole neighborhood like a 7.9 on the Richter scale. Dimitri's lawyer went down. His bodyguards run and grab Dimitri to safety. Not too far behind the lawyer, Val's body was lifeless lying on the ground looking pure white. The glass had torn through some of her flesh. Her body was positioned where shinny sharp glass could be seen clinging to her body. Agents came flying out looking up and around. They see a black van and try to locate a license plate. It looks like someone had taken and stripped it right off the vehicle. They all ran back towards Agent Val. Someone called the paramedic because they had an agent down. Val was rushed to the hospital. They immediately transport her in the back getting her ready for surgery. Miller, Casey, and her Boss rushed by her side.

Chase (called Miller- he heard about Agent Val): *"Is she okay?"*

"No one came out yet to explain anything to us, however: we'll let you know the outcome.

"Thank you, Sir."

Miller (talking to Casey): *"Chase heard about Agent Val. He called to see if she's okay. Does anyone know anything about the lawyer? They say he is in surgery as well. Casey, do you have any ideas about who could have done this?"*

"YES, I do, Left-hand Blaze. This has his name written all over it. His aim was Dimitri, but he got away; Dimitri is far from being done."

The word got back to Blaze that there was an attempt on Dimitri's life, but he got away. A phone call came in to Russia; it is Left-hand Blaze. He wants to know who the hell is Dimitri Father. The only way to find out would be to call him.

"What can I do for you? I heard about the attempt on your son's life this morning."

{Nothing gets past me, Mr. Blaze you do not want to make an enemy out of me; your little business is no match compared to me. That is something that can be deleted into never existing. I am a very messy person. I can also get the job done without any interference. I hope

you're catching on? Instead of me ending your small business, why
don't we make a deal."}

*"...and what would that be? I can have your son killed before he even gets
home. We can talk about that Mister. It is not just me you must worry
about. It is the Mafia, cartels, it's every damn body that dealt with your son
and everything is far from being over. Everyone that has or has been doing
business with Dimitri is after him. To end this, I'll send you my account
number and you have one hour to put back the money I had to send out
because of your son. Not only that, but a little extra for the energy I had
to put out there for your prick of a son you've raised. By the way, you need
to train your son if he wants this lifestyle, it is not useful to con people that
can pave his way in this business. While I am living, your son Dimitri will
never be able to grow what you've built because of his greed; one hour."*

Click....dial tone. Blaze pressure was boiling to 250* Celsius. He
hangs up the phone. His right-hand man Ron was standing by. Blaze
gets a nod from Ron saying the money is in the account. Then, there
was a loud knock-on Blaze's front door.

OPEN UP CIA.

Blaze's butler answers the door, but before he could open the front
door, the CIA busted inside while Blaze was walking out.

"What seems to be the problem? Why are you all damaging my home?"

"Sir, you are under arrest."

"ARREST? for what?"

"For the attempted murder of an Agent and Lawyer."

"Call my lawyer."

"Will do, Sir."

Blaze's lawyer gets there before he is brought down to Langley and she waits on them to bring him.

"She's Handling My Case."

"Deputy, Blaze is my client."

Blaze takes a seat. They handcuff and shackle him to the chair.

"What are you doing? Why are you trying to kill those people?"

"Bella, you know me. I don't leave trails."

"Listen. I have to get you in and out of here before someone sees me. We have bail. They have no proof. They arrested you based on speculation."

Before Casey and Miller were able to question Blaze, his bond was set at 1.5 million dollars.

"Dammit, we cannot even catch a break with this man."

Miller gets a phone call that Agent Val is out of surgery.

"Sir, have they heard anything about Dimitri Lawyer?"

"Um yeah, he didn't make it."

They rush down to see Agent Val.

"You all can have a short visit, but please do not stay long. She has a long road ahead of her, but she is going to make it with a lot of rest and NO excitement."

"What did you have to do to her?"

"We had to repair her lungs. She has a few broken ribs and a fractured ankle. We also had to take out a lot of shrapnel. The other person that was also in the incident didn't make it. His lungs were damaged from the shrapnel. It pierced through his body. They are sending his things up here."

As they walk in, they see she is still sleeping. The anesthesia has not worn off yet. The nurse comes in to check her vital signs. A few minutes later, she wakes up, looks at everyone, her face lights up with a smile. She spoke.

Val (whispering softly): "...*hi guys*...(long pause with deep breaths) *You did not have to come.*"

"*Save your energy. We will check on you later.*"

As they walk out they can hear her talking barely.

"*Thanks guys, it means a lot to me. She went back out like a light.*"

"*Sir, I don't know anything about Agent Val. Does she have a family we need to contact?*"

"*She keeps that side a secret. She barely talks about her family.*"

A few minutes later Big Ronnie walks in to pay his respects to the Agent and to see how she is doing. She was sleeping, but before he walked out, she woke up.

Val (groggy): "*Hey*"

Big Ronnie (turning back around excitedly): "*Hey there! I heard about what happened and thought I would come to see how you are doing. Get some sleep. I will be checking in on you if you don't mind from time to time.*"

Casey saw Big Ronnie walking out of Agent Val's room. He is wondering what that was all about. There is more to Agent Val than they all know. As he walks up to Miller and NSA Director Val's boss, they receive the lawyer's things and his cell phone. Before they left, they told Agent Val's doctor that they were picking up Agent Val's bill. The doctor told them someone already paid for it in full.

"By whom may I ask?"

"Her brother."

"I never knew she had a brother, but she doesn't talk about her family. She's very private. When the time comes, she'll open up."

Casey (remembers seeing Big Ronnie walking out of her room): *"It can't be... Big Ronnie is her brother. That is why he came to the courtroom with the video."*

They walk back to the office. Miller gave Casey the day off.

"Report back to work tomorrow at 0800 hundred hours. We need those explosives. The conference call with the Secretary of State is in the morning."

Casey gets a phone call. His mother is back in town.

"Mother, when did you get in? I'll stop by later on tomorrow to see how you're doing."

{"Hello son. Oh I got in yesterday afternoon just before 2pm. Casey, I have another engagement to attend so how about I met you while I'm in town for a quick bit to eat. Let's say around 1pm."}

"That sounds good to me."

He hangs up with his mother not suspecting she is meeting with her client Blaze. She was talking over some strategies about his case. Little did she know they caught Blaze hands stuck in the cookie jar of illegal activity. How is he going to get out of this mess?

"Mr. Blaze, can you tell me why they arrested you in the first place? They are saying that you were under arrest for attempted murder, treason and ect."

"I didn't do this."

"*Can you tell me who it could be, they think you've murdered someone?*"

"*Some people that I sold some items to online knew that Dimitri double-crossed me. Everyone knows he has gotten himself arrested. They heard Dimitri has Diplomatic Immunity. No one knew he even had Diplomatic Immunity. The next day he was out. He has my money and the items we sold on the internet.*"

"*Aha, are you referring to these explosives?*"

"*YEAH! how did you know?*"

"*I know a lot. I've also heard of what's been going on with you as well, Blaze.*"

"*Dimitri dad gave me a call threatening me. I told him that his son is still here in the US and that I could have his son killed before he gets home. Dimitri's father paid me back with interest. I'm guessing someone has a hit on Dimitri. Maybe it's the people who thought they were going to get the explosives. I have already paid them back to keep them off my ass. Those people want those explosives. It is not even about the money. They would rather have those explosives than the money. I was able to settle my accounts in full and his father paid me. Why would I go and kill Dimitri. Let's be smart about this!*"

"*Well Mr. Blaze, you need to find out who and why they tried to kill Dimitri, or you are going to be in the media for months for this. I am no longer doing cases because I am retired. The person I trained will be your lawyer in court. I will be something like your counselor. Blaze, I will have your lawyer call you tomorrow. We will talk soon. Good day sir.*"

"*Ok Counselor. I will take you for your word.*"

Bella walks into the restaurant to meet her son for lunch.

"Mother, how's auntie doing?"

"She is doing well. She has cats to keep her company. She says hello by the way."

"When did you get back? 2 days ago, I presume? Hope everything is ok…"

"Yeah, I have a case. They called me in to handle this case. It was by request. It is nothing I cannot handle, son."

Casey's phone rings. It is Miller.

{"Casey, I need you back at the office."}

"Mother, they need me back at the office. Maybe we can pick this up another day."

"Of course. "Bye son.

Casey kisses his mother on the cheek. A few hours later, he walks into the office. Miller is talking to Chase. He is back.

"Chase, welcome back, is everything okay?"

"Yeah, I'm back. Everything is as well as can be expected."

"Casey, Chase is the head agent at ATF now."

"Damn Chase, congrats. Why are you here?"

"Chase is taking the place of Val so you both will be working together. He will report back to me. The CIA is the lead agent on this case."

"Yes Sir."

Chase and Casey had much caught up to do. Casey never told Chase how much he appreciated the help on getting him started in the right direction on the case. They went out for a few beers.

"Chase, how is it on the other side of the tracks?"

"We'll see, with me just getting started, I'll let you know. Miller caught me up to speed on what is going on, he also told me about Val."

"Yeah Chase, it was bad."

"Dimitri got away with his diplomatic immunity papers that we never knew he had. He is on his way back to Russia. I told Miller about Dimitri's father. Blaze was not the person who threw that bomb. It was someone who he double-crossed before he betrayed Blaze. They called in ATF. Val is going to be out for a while, so they gave me a promotion for what happened in Afghanistan. The Lead agent for ATF knows about Alek helping Dimitri. They also killed the cook Walter, Tracy Fletcher's brother."

"Chase, do you know where she is?"

"We are still working on that. We are going to head into where Dimitri's father has his son. Dimitri's father has him lying low in another country. We must bring him back to pay for all this confusion he has caused. He is in Budapest, and we leave tomorrow. Miller already knows that we will meet up at Langley at 0500 hundred hours."

"I'll see you all tomorrow."

They clink bottles and enjoy the rest of their evening. The next morning, they are leaving for Budapest. When they walk in, Miller and the Attorney General greet them both.

"Casey, meet the Attorney General. You will be reporting to him now through me."

Casey shakes his hand.

"I have heard so much about you. We would not have gotten this far if it were not for you. I wanted to meet you and shake your hand and to say

thank you. Now we need Dimitri back by any means and I do not care how he gets back here."

"I was glad to help Sir."

"Nevertheless, it's good to have you on our team."

"Chase, I thought Dimitri has Diplomatic immunity."

"Yes, he does. The Attorney General said to let him worry about that and just bring him in for questioning."

They flew out for Budapest. Chase and Casey reached their destination safely. Dimitri was believed to be in Hungary. They got information from secret intelligence service that Alek was killed outside of Hungary. They are gunning for Dimitri and whoever it is wants those explosives that he still has in his possession. When Chase and Casey touched down in Budapest, someone met them to take them the rest of the way. When they reached Hungary, they made a stop at the site looking for clues on Alek's death. They were hoping they could find something that would link them to who was doing all of this. Chase picks up some custom-made bullet casings. He also spots some tobacco from the cigar and a Julio Cesar wrapping paper from the butt of the cigar that was left behind on the ground.

"Are we looking at Mexican cartels? Can't help but think all this just keeps getting interesting. Who else did he piss off and is all of this just for money? No, I do not believe so Casey. I think he is in this just for the fun of it."

"Does he need money? His father is a well-known Mafia back In Russia. We need to think about how we are going to take Dimitri down without anyone knowing his gone."

"Casey, I think we need to put the Colombian Cartels down. They are just going to fellow Dimitri wherever he goes. I have some friends I can call. They owe me a favor. Give me a minute."

Chase made a few phone calls. They made their way to a villa inside Hungary.

"Wait here Casey."

Chase walks in then walks right back out. They head out to find Dimitri. Chase big favor came through. He received the phone call and was on stand-by. They head outside of the city. Chase got another phone call telling him the Colombian Cartels are there as well.

"Casey, are you straped?"

"Yeah, why wouldn't I be?"

"Good. We are going to have some company."

They walk up to an abandoned building. Guns drawn; Chase friends walk up on the side of them. Casey was looking around wondering what their location was.

"Casey, we do not have much time. Spread out everyone. We need to find Dimitri."

They hear someone in the back.... over there....surrounding Dimitri with a gun.

"Man, you both never give up. I have...."

"Yes, we know...Diplomatic Immunity."

"Dimitri, put the gun down."

"Hell NO! You are not taking me back. I am not going to prison!"

"You need to be accountable for those things. Besides, we are not the only ones you pissed off. You know the Colombians are in town and they are coming to collect your ass. You can either go with us or wait for your friends; it's your call."

Chase gets a phone call letting him know the Cartels are on the way.

"Did you hear that Dimitri. Your friends are coming; it's either now or never?"

Dimitri puts the gun down just in time. Cars begin pulling up.

"Damn, Casey, where are you? Are you right behind me brother? I cannot move. They are everywhere!"

"Damn, we need to force our way out. We have a pickup in 3 hours and if we are not there the next pick up won't be till the next 48 hours."

Chase's friends called for more help. They came in with grenades and were throwing them everywhere, blowing up cars. They ran to the car and drove off. Colombians were right behind them. Chase was behind the steering wheel and Casey was slinging bullets, throwing grenades.

"Casey holds on, hard right turn!!!"

As Casey holds on. Bullets were flying piercing everything in their way. Dimitri ducks off behind the seats. Chase's friends were throwing grenades and blowing up cars. Suddenly, a sniper starts taking them down one by one until it was just the head Colombian Cartel left. The vehicles suddenly stopped. They had him surrounded without any doubt. They walk up to him and threaten him. They let him know that if he were to follow them, he would never see the light of day again. Chase turns around and retreats. The Cartel took his gun out and before he could shoot Chase, Casey shot him. Chase converses with Casey that it was good looking out.

"Dimitri, you've pissed off many people. So tell us, is there anyone else we need to worry about? What did you do to the Colombians? Casey, how long do we have?"

"1.5 hours Chase. Let us make this count."

They had a 2-hour drive but only 1.5 hours for pick up.

"Okay let's go!"

Before leaving, Chase thanked his friends and waved goodbye.

"Casey, how good are you at driving?"

"They used to call me Tokyo Drift."

"Yeah right…whatever you say. Well come on, Mr. Tokyo, let's ride. Casey, let's see what you got. Make a right and drive 20 kilometers, then turn left and at 120 kilometers turn left. Come on Casey faster…punch it 50 kilometers…turn left again…hit it Casey."

Casey was at an expert mark driving 125mph.

"150 kilometers turn right…come on Dammit…we're not going to make it. Casey, we need to make this flight. I thought they called you Tokyo…"

"Chase you are being a smartass right now."

"I do not want to wait another 48 hours. I would like to be in my own home sipping on some good Cognac."

They barely made it. The plane was just getting ready to take off. Everyone got on safely. Everyone was told to rest. They had an 18-hour flight home. The conference call came through. It was Miller and the Attorney General.

"Yes Sir."

Attorney General: {"I heard congratulations are in order to you both. You got Dimitri. Arrive home safely."}

"Roger that Sir!"

Attorney General: {"Chase, we would not have Dimitri if it were not for you."}

They made it back home with Dimitri. Entering the US at Langley, they brought him in. The Attorney General made a few phone calls and Dimitri Diplomatic Immunity was getting revoked so he could get charged. Miller gave Casey that day off. Casey made it his business to stop by to see Val. When he got there, Casey saw Big Ronnie coming out. He walks in the room. Casey pulls out a chair to sit by her side. Val woke up to Casey sleeping. She smiles and gives Casey a nudge. Casey wakes up to Val's smile.

"Hi Val."

"Casey, what a surprise."

"Why would it be a surprise, Val? We worked together and you got hurt in the line of duty. I am not going to abandon you because you got hurt. So, tell me how you are feeling? Have the doctors said when you're able to leave the hospital?"

"They are saying that if I keep doing better, I will be able to leave in two days."

"You gave us quite a scare Val. I am so glad you are doing much better. I see that you had company. Big Ronnie was here."

"Oh yeah, he stops by sometimes to check in on me."

"Can you tell me how and who he is to you?"

"Ronnie is my orphan brother. We grew up in the system. He is like my adoptive big brother but we are not blood-related. He looks after me like I am his little sister."

"Can I ask for a favor?"

"Yeah, sure."

"Do you think you could arrange a meeting for me and Big Ronnie? I have many questions that haven't been answered and giving the agency an update would help out, but also to keep us from wasting time. We are staggering into something we all don't know that much about or what's taking place... I was wondering if..."

Val (interrupting): *"Say no more Casey. I will talk to him."*

"Have Big Ronnie call me, and I could meet him, or he can come down to my office."

"No problem. I'll make sure he gets the message."

"Thanks and get some rest. I will come back to check on you in a few days."

Casey walks out and runs into Chase and Miller.

"Hey, how is Val doing?"

"She's going to recover. Go in... she will be happy to see you both."

Casey stops by to see Bella. As he walks in, she is doing her norm. The house is smelling so good. Casey glides over to her pot.

"Mother, I know what you are doing. What's on the stove?"

He sticks a spoon inside her pot. If his mother catches him he knew what she was going to do. She walks in.

"Your fav... macaroni and cheese and my fried chicken. Are you staying for dinner?

Her eyes open wide as she walks over and pops him on his hand.

Bella (pausing): "CASEY!! What have I told you about my pots? Did you wash up? NO! Now are you staying for dinner or not?"

"Ma, you are the only woman I know that can handle me.... (grinning) Why would you ask me that? Of course I'm staying."

"Go and get washed up then!"

They sit down to dinner.

"Is there anything new going on?"

"Just working on a case."

"Is everything okay with the case?"

"Yeah. Just trying to give him some counseling!"

"Mother, if you need anything let me know."

Casey kisses Bella good night and closes the door. The next morning Casey phone rings. It was Val.

{"Good morning, Casey. Can you stop by the hospital before work?"}

"I could come to say around 0700 hundred hours."

Casey gets up to start his day. He walks into Val's room.

"Good morning!"

Casey sees a tall, medium-built man. He thinks it is Big Ronnie. He walks over towards the man and shakes his hand.

"Hey, Big Ronnie I'm assuming...I need to ask you a few questions if you don't mind. Can we step outside? I need to know what made you buy into the auction Blaze had going?"

"I wanted him to know the clout that I have. My pockets are very deep."

"Who told the Colombians how to get Dimitri?"

"I knew a few people. I just made a few calls."

"Dimitri killed Walter because he was snooping around Blaze estate. He blew him up in that shed he had him tied up in. I have eyes all over. Blaze just doesn't know who I have in my pocket."

"Do you know why Tracy Fletcher left?"

"I don't know for sure. But there was talk about her and her brother having a plan that, if for some apparent reason he doesn't answer any of her phone calls, something went wrong somewhere. I think she was supposed to move on and not look back. That's the word that is going around."

"Do you know what she did? Do you know where she is?"

"The last time I heard she was in Budapest."

"Damn, I knew I saw her there. Thanks for your help Big Ronnie."

That morning Casey went to work. He knew they had Dimitri out right.

"Miller, Sir I found out that Dimitri killed Walter, Tracy Fletcher's brother. That is enough to revoke his immunity and have him charged with murder."

The Attorney General calls the State Department in Dimitri's home country to waive immunity for one Dimitri Petrov. When the call came in, Dimitri's father was already alerted about his son. Before Casey went home, he decided to stop back by to see Val at the hospital.

"Hello, Casey, I am packing my things so I can go back to my apartment."

"If you need me in the morning, let me know. I can take you home."

"I think I will stay in the apartment they rented for the case. The contract ends at the last day of this month."

"No worries. If you need anything, I am next door. Just remember that whenever they release you."

Casey walks out and his phone rings. It's Big Ronnie wanting to meet up with him.

"There is some news going around the Syndicate crime families about Dimitri."

"Meet me at the coffee shop down the street from Langley around 0900 hundred hours."

Casey is worked up over what was going on over the past few days. He was pumped up to the point that he did a full body workout. He woke up the next morning at the crack of dawn. Getting ready for his jog early that morning always seems to clear his mind. That always seems to get him thinking clearly. Casey rushes upstairs to the front door from his long run. He placed his Danish and orange juice for breakfast on a brown hardwood table inside the outer room from the kitchen. His small special place has a banquette facing across the street from his kitchen. Overlooking the female doctor with the long legs, who just moved in across the street. Casey was just in time as he watched his neighbor through the window. Angela's legs were all muscle, pushing and pulling and working with signs of fatigue. As Casey watches her running on a treadmill; if she ever had to escape a lunatic, his money would be on Angela. Casey had his excitement for the morning. He jumps in the shower to meet with Big Ronnie at the coffee shop. He arrives early waiting patiently. Big Ronnie walks up, grabs a cup of coffee, then walks over to where Casey was. They both sit down.

"Casey, the only reason I am giving you information is because of my little sister. I care so much about Val. Now here goes .... Dimitri not only pissed off the Colombian Cartel but he also pissed off the Mexican Cartels!"

"WHAT? DAMN... If it's not the Mafias and the Cartels!"

CHAPTER FOUR

Mission Out of Control

DIMITRI'S FATHER WAS on the warpath. He sent his men and another lawyer to the US. Attorney General and Miller both wait for the paperwork to come in from Russia. They delay as long as they can, but nothing happens. The Attorney General made a phone call telling them to get his plane ready because he needs to make a trip outside the US. Miller went along for the ride and for backup. They both entered the plane. The Attorney General told Miller that they were on their way to Russia to have a man to man talk with Dimitri's father.

Miller and Attorney General lands in Russia 15 hours later. They had a car on standby at the airport. They are having a meeting with Dimitri's father at the American embassy. Dimitri's father walks in and the Embassy explains he was on American soil. He walks in asking them what they wanted.

"If you are here for me to tell them to waive my son's immunity then you are wasting your time. You're worried about my son; you need to worry about Vashi lyudi." (In Russian-your people)

"What did he say in his conversation?"

American Embassy: *"Sir, he is saying 'your people'!"*

Miller makes a call and finds out that Langley is under attack, They could not believe that was happening on American soil. They need to cut their visit short to make their way back to the US. Miller and the Attorney General rush back. Casey and Chase were inside Langley. They had Dimitri in the basement in a cell.

"Chase, they are here for Dimitri, they are trying to take him back home. They are determined."

"I think you should say his father is Determined. We need to get some weapons out of the weapon storage room."

They head to the second floor using the stairs. They see more men coming in from off the top room coming on the same level they are on.

"Dammit, we need more ammunition. We need to take them out."

One of the men walked to the back of the room and the other one walked on the other side. Chase walked to the other end as soon as the guy walked out. Chase kicks him in the face, sweeps him from under his feet, and puts him in a chokehold until he is unconscious. He bound him, taped his mouth up, and stuffed him in a closet. Casey caught his guy coming out and hit him in the head with the butt of his gun. Casey tapes his legs, ties his hands behind his back, and tapes up his mouth after he stuffed something inside. He drags him to the closet. They hear a noise in the hallway as they walk out. Chase and Casey see two more men down on the other end with guns in their hands.

"Let's go on the other end and see if we can cut them off on the other side."

Casey motioned his acknowledgement with a nod. They both began running just in time. They caught them both. Casey runs and jumps up with a kick and knocks one of the bad guys out. The other guy who was with him pulls out his gun just in time. Chase jolt the weapon out of his hand and sweeps his feet from under him. The guy falls to the floor and Chase jabs him with his elbow. They tie and gag them both and place them inside the storage room standing upright.

"There are too many of them. Four down and ten more to go. We need some help. Let's split up."

Casey went to the next floor and Chase stayed on that floor. Casey saw a man looking in each room making sure that each room was empty. Casey grabs a sparkling cider bottle, throws it across the room, and hits the bad guy in the back of his head. The man develops a goose egg on the back of his head the size of a lemon. He walks up to the other one and sidekicks him in the back. The man springs forward and runs towards Casey with a knife. Casey uses his hands to block the blade from cutting him. Casey kicks him, breaking his kneecap. The man falls to the floor. Casey ties him up. He gags both of their mouths and locks them in the bathroom.

Chase and Casey heard a helicopter touchdown on their rooftop of the old Langley building; it was their boss Miller along with more agents. Three men had already entered the building sent by retired Russian Mafia Dimitri's father. Looking for Dimitri, they made their way down toward the basement, arriving just in time. Shooting off the lock from his jail cell door, Dimitri walks out and grabs a gun. His father decided to send his plane. He made sure he had a private aircraft waiting out on a small, abandoned airfield. Miller and his agents were working their way towards Casey and Chase. The door flew open.

Miller and his agents entered the room handing Casey and Chase more ammunition for their weapons.

"Miller, how did you find out Langley was down?"

"His father told us. He is the one who sent these men to break Dimitri out. The Attorney General has returned to Washington, DC. He is still trying to get Dimitri's immunity revoked."

"Will Dimitri still be standing trial for the killing in Syria? Sir, he needs to pay for his crime."

"We are currently having issues. (Sighs then pause) It is taking us longer than we expected. We might lose this battle."

Casey (interrupted): *"What do you mean losing this battle?"*

"His father is not giving up his son, not without a fight. Shhh, I hear them coming."

Miller, Casey, and Chase have them surrounded by their agents.

Miller (authoritative): *"PUT YOUR WEAPONS DOWN!"*

Dimitri (stern): *"WHY? No one is going to stop us. We are getting out of here today. You put down YOUR gun"*

As they move around the room getting in a better position, Dimitri spots Miller along with Casey and Chase. A shot was fired from Dimitri gun aiming for their heads. Chase and Casey were crouching down to the floor near the filing cabinet. Bullets start flying everywhere. Miller rolls on the floor lying down beside a brown marble desk.

They all tread warily.

Dimitri (yelling across the room): *"Do you like that?"* (reprimanding from across the room)

"You need to turn yourself in."

"Not a chance Bubba."

Chase is trying to run for cover, but sees an opportunity and gets close to Dimitri.

Dimitri (looking in Chase eyes): *"You are still not even close enough. I will kill you with a blink of an eye!"*

Dimitri shot a round of bullets trying to aim for Chase and Casey. As Dimitri takes cover to protect himself from being harmed, one of his men threw a knife over towards him for extra protection. Chase saw the exchange, ran up, and knocks Dimitri down. Dimitri looks up and turns around with a sidekick that knocks Chase out. Casey and Miller saw Chase getting his butt knocked out. They ran over to check his pulse. Dimitri ran towards an exit trying to escape to the next floor. Casey shot at the door before Dimitri was able to exit. Dimitri ducks off behind a desk looking over towards Casey and Miller. They took a shot at Dimitri, but he has a gun in his hand and he takes a shot back at them. Miller and Casey duck off. Chase, being weary, wakes up nodding his head back and forth just in the nick of time. He gets up and takes a swing at Dimitri and misses. Dimitri laughs it off. One of Dimitri's men threw over another weapon.

"You are no match for me. We can go on all day. (Yelling out loud) *You see my men are very loyal and we came well equipped."*

He throws a smoke bomb and starts shooting. The shots were coming fast and steady. This time he was using an M489 light machine gun while running to the door. Chase jumps up and shoots Dimitri in the leg. Dimitri fell to the floor. He was in excruciating pain. He started suddenly speaking Russian.

"What did you just do to me?"

He covered his eyes to keep from seeing all the blood rushing to the floor.

Dmitri (yelling over and over): *"You shot me in my leg!"*

He was feeling nauseous and sweaty holding the gunshot wound so that he would not lose too much blood. His hands are covered with blood as he looks over at Chase.

"You're going to pay for this."

Casey came up and took the gun away from Dimitri. Chase looked him in his eyes.

Chase (excited): *"No, you are going to pay in that jail cell."*

Chase handcuffs Dimitri. The agents escort all of them down into the cell. EMS was dispatched out. They had an agent accompanying Dimitri to the hospital. Word got back home to his father that his son was captured and taken to the hospital. They still have not obtained those papers from his country revoking his immunity. His father already started setting up plans. With his father's powerful political pull, he paid the doctor and nurses that were doing Dimitri procedure to help his son escape. His father also had someone to pose as a CIA agent to deport the guys in the basement back to Russia.

Chase and Casey waited for Dimitri to come out of surgery. Two hours later, still no Dimitri. The guys went into the recovery room. Rumors spread throughout the hospital and within the agencies on duty. Dimitri had escaped and was no longer there. Miller puts the hospital on lockdown. He sent some of the agents all through the hospital, but they could not find Dimitri. Miller calls the Attorney

General letting him know that Dimitri had gotten away again. This time, his father is not going to take his freedom lightly. He brought Dimitri back home somewhere in the mountains in Russia, which is where Dimitri is laying low for now.

Back at Langley, Miller, Chase and Casey are having a video conference with Attorney General and the Secretary of State.

"When we find Dimitri's whereabouts, we will notify you. Immunity is not going to happen unless Dimitri's father slips up and frankly, I don't see that happening anytime soon. Miller, I will stay in touch with you."

"Yes, Sir Attorney General. Okay guys, you heard the Attorney General and the Secretary of the State. You both can take the day off. Stop by to see Val because they are releasing her today. Maybe you two muscular young men can take her home.

"But Sir, with so much at stake, we do not need to take an entire day off!"

"Take the day off because there is nothing more you can do here until we find out where Dimitri is. We will keep you guys posted. Report back here 0800 hundred hours."

Casey and Chase stopped by to pick up some flowers for Val. They also started browsing for a stuffed animal before heading to the hospital.

"Chase, are you well connected with any connections in Russia?"

"My friends are extremely limited in Russia but I will make a few phone calls."

Chase steps away to give his wife a call.

"Alexa, is there anything you can find out about where Dimitri is, or can you get me some of your connections over in Russia?"

{"Give me an hour or two."}

They both pull up at the hospital. Val is in her room packing. Her back turned from the door.

"I am here to pick up a Valarie?"

She turns around smiles, hugging them both.

"It is the guys... CASEY, CHASE. How are you guys doing? I heard Dimitri had Langley on lockdown. Are you guys, okay? Tell me what happened."

While Casey explains the details to her, Chase has another phone call. His wife was calling back.

"Alexa, what did you find out?"

{"It's going to take a little longer; probably around another hour tops. Will you be home for dinner tonight?"}

Before he could answer, Casey came out the door with some of Val's things.

{"I hear the noise. I take it you are busy. I will give you a call back in another hour or two."}

Chase hangs up and helps Casey take the rest of Val's things to the car. Big Ronnie shows up and Val walks up towards Ronnie to tell him that they released her from the hospital and the guys were taking her home. She also welcomes Big Ronnie to stop by as well. As they pull up to Val's apartment grabbing her things as she settles in, Big Ronnie pulls up and walks in with bags of food from Val's favorite restaurant; Carlito. Big Ronnie brought enough for everyone.

Before Chase's wife could call him back, the Attorney General gave Miller a call back notifying him about Dimitri and his whereabouts.

Miller informs the guys that Dimitri's father sent him to Budapest until he was able to finish building a small cabin for Dimitri in Khibiny Mountain. It was going to be a difficult mission getting to him. This time of year it is snowing. If they were to go in his country and pull him out of there, they were going to need more workforce. As they were all in a meeting, Alexa calls to notify Chase what she found out. It was somewhat similar to what the Attorney General briefing was, but she adds that they could go in as tourists/visitors.

{"You all could go in and do a private Russian guided tour of Khibiny because it is the biggest mountain of the Kola peninsula. You could do a snowmobile tour or a Husky safari tour. We would have some men ready and waiting. It will be even harder to locate Dimitri because his father has him tucked somewhere up in the mountains."}

Later, Casey briefs everyone on his conversation with Big Ronnie. Casey receives a text from Val telling him to give her a call. Casey steps out the room to place a phone call

Casey: *"Val, this Casey. Is there anything wrong?"*

{"Big Ronnie called giving me an update. Tracy Fletcher left Budapest. She couldn't even trust anyone. Big Ronnie got a call from her with details about a black book that she has that Walter kept up with Blaze and Dimitri missions and whereabouts. She's in Romania living with the money that her and Walter had saved up for another life. Big Ronnie also found out that Dimitri's father cut him off from the family business and fortune. Dimitri is going around selling and taking back the explosives so he could start his empire with the money he is taking and leaving behind a trail of pissed off Mafias and Cartels after his father cut him out of the business."}

"I wonder if his father knows about his plan? If Tracy Fletcher has enough on Dimitri, that could be what we need to bring him back the proper way. This time it is going to be a little bit trickier because of his whereabouts but could it be that easy?"

Miller calls his agents Casey and Chase telling them to report back to work 0600 hundred hours. As Casey and Chase walked to their cars, they decide to see if they could go to Romania to find Tracy Fletcher. They end up telling director Miller everything they know.

Chase and Casey depart the company for the evening. Casey walks into his apartment building. Val is still getting her rest. He meditates for half a night then he goes out jogging to the gym for 2300 hours. He walks through the door. His smooth masculine body is soaking wet. He walks to the bathroom getting ready to take a shower. He takes one look in the mirror with his green eyes at his thin masculine sweaty face and realizes that his wavy hair is getting thick and in need of a haircut.

The next morning, Casey awakes at 0400 hundred hours and begins getting ready for work. Val still is not up. He walks up to her door and places his ear up against the door. He realizes it is quiet and that she is getting her rest. Later, Chase sees Casey at the coffee shop. They both walked in at 0530 hours. Miller was already in and it looks like he never left. You would never know Miller even had a home, or he just does not go there. Chase and Casey decide to have a talk with Miller about the case. They felt like the most important thing they needed to do right then and there was to get Tracy Fletcher back to the US. They explain that she is the key to the whole case. After picking her up, They could then go for Dimitri if the Mexican Cartels had not gotten to him yet.

"If that's the case, we need not waste any more time. I will send the coordinates to you. Someone will meet you at the airfield after you arrive. Good luck."

Miller arranges the flight for Romania. Casey and Chase finally made it to Budapest. Everything felt like Walter and Tracy had all this planned a long time ago. They wanted a place in Romania, which was far away from the United States. They start in the area where Casey saw her, thinking that they would be able to run into her again. Time had gone and Casey did not think she was even around any longer.

"Hey Chase, can you find your friends from the last time we were here?"

Chase made some phone calls to Szia Istvan Araki (Hello Istvan Araki) Chase speaking in Hungarian as he walked off speaking in Hungarian.

Chase (walking back toward Casey): *"Casey, I got a friend. He will be here in a few minutes".*

A young man walks up saying Szia,

"Istvan hogy vagy?" (How have you been)

As they both speak in English.

"Istvan, we are looking for a young lady; American in her early 30's, Burnett hair, 5'6, 125lbs, brown eyes…she was here awhile back while we were trying to bring Dimitri back. We're thinking she had someone helping her. We are trying to locate her whereabouts. We think she may have left for Romania, but we are not sure where in Romania. You think you could help us out?"

"Chase, let me see what I can find out."

"Istvan, you will be well compensated."

"Give me half a day. I will try to find her whereabouts."

Casey (walks up to Chase): *"It never seems to amaze me how well rounded you are. You have so many different languages under your belt…"*

"You have been out of the game. When did you retire?"

"2 years Chase!"

"You retired right before I left for Budapest. I was on a mission deep undercover for a year. That is when I learned. After that I left for Afghanistan for a year. I was just getting back home when this mission came up. They put me on the Red Dawn Case."

Casey was taking his time. He really was getting to know the man whom he was trusting with his life.

"Tell me Casey, do you regret IT …?"

"Regret what?"

"RETIRING!"

"I do miss traveling around the world."

Chase phone rings. It is Istvan.

"What have you found out?"

{"She is in a small town called Deva in Romania. You can travel by car. She works in a little restaurant named Capriccio Deva. Here is the address. It opens at 10am. If you leave now, you will be able to get some rest just before her shift begins."}

Casey and Chase leave. It is about a six hour drive. They chose to split the ride and were wondering who would be driving the first shift. They arrived there two hours before the restaurant opened. After stopping by the restaurant, they found Tracy Fletcher was not due to report to work until 1200 hundred hours. They both conclude to get a couple of rooms to rest and freshen up a little. They found a hotel near the restaurant, and after getting settled in, Casey went jogging. Casey spots Tracy shopping. He follows her from each store until she goes to her place of residence. Casey jogs back to the hotel. As he walked in, Chase was already waiting on him. Casey explains to Chase he spotted Tracy out shopping and that he followed her. Casey freshens up some as he and Chase walks out the door. They ran over to get a peep and a bite to eat at the Capriccio Deva restaurant where Tracy worked. They waited for her shift to begin and they watched Tracy during her shift. Tracy had a feeling someone was watching her. She walks towards the kitchen, snatches her bag, and runs out into the back ally. Just so happened, Casey was waiting for her. She was shocked and surprised to see Casey.

Tracy (murmuring): *"Casey, what are you doing here?"*

"We came to bring you back home. I had a talk with Big Ronnie. He told me about the little black book your brother kept up with Dimitri and Blaze moves. We need that book!"

"You need what?"

"We are bringing you back in for treason!"

"Like hell you are. If that is the case, then I don't have the black book."

Casey (disturbed): *"What do you mean you do not have the book?"*

"Casey, that is my bargaining chip. When you give me what I want, then we can talk."

"Tracy Fletcher, what is it that you want?"

"Protection Program...do not tell me that it's impossible and that it does not apply to me. I know you can make it happen. If you try to take me out of this country, I'll scream bloody murder until they arrest you both for kidnapping. If you had a warrant for my arrest, we wouldn't be sitting here chit chatting. You would've had the Serviciul de Informatii Externe (SIE/ Foreign Intelligence Service), but you don't, which makes me think you don't have a warrant for my arrest or even the right credentials to take me out of this country. Before I would allow you to touch me and drag me through this country, I would slice off each of your fingers every time you reach for me. Do not get it twisted."

Tracy walks off. Chase comes from the front to see her. Casey then walks behind her and stops her to finish talking. He strikes up a deal with her letting her know that he could get her into the program.

Chase (looking at Casey confused): *"Casey, what in the hell are you doing?"*

"They will make a deal with her because all the things she has done do not compare to what Dimitri has done. We lose a fish, and we gain a whale."

"This book will not leave my side until then. You know where you can find me, good day gentlemen."

Tracy walks off back to her shift feeling very confident. Chase jumps on the phone with the Secretary of the State and the Attorney General. Chase is turning heads and making it happen, but it will take a while. Meanwhile, they are watching Tracy, making sure she does not leave. Tracy walks up to them out of the blue to let them know that she is watching them as well.

"They found your brother's remains. Dimitri killed him. He was snooping around Blaze's property."

Tracy (talking to them both): *"Do you both think this is going to make a difference? I still want the witness protection program. I have the book, and I have looked at the things they have done. Dimitri is a psychopath and Blaze isn't any better. I've made plenty of copies and they are in a safe place. If I get screwed, that will be my life insurance, or if you prefer, my bargaining chip. My brother taught me well; along with the agency."*

She walks off to her place even more assured and left them outside, overseeing her home.

"Casey, she is not going anywhere. She is in a low key. She knows her best options is the program."

They went back to the hotel to wait on word back from home and the documents to show proof of putting Tracy in the witness protection program. Casey decides to get cleaned up and get that haircut he's been trying to get for days. Chase phone rings. Miller on the other end.

"Miller Sir."

{*"The program has been approved for one Tracy Fletcher. Chase, you can bring her in. Sending papers through your phone."*}

Chase and Casey pack their things and rush over to pick up Tracy, but when they get there, she is nowhere to be found.

"Dammit she's gone again; Tracy Fletcher is on the run!"

"She can't be far. She must still be in the country. We know she's going to need some help."

Chase made a phone call to his friend Istvan. As Istvan picks up, Chase tells him that they think Tracy Fletcher ran and could he have found out from his resource her location

Istvan: {*"Give me 30 min."*}

Chase and Casey search through the room for clues on where she could have gone. Casey picks up a paper pad that he could tell she used it to write on. He took a pencil and sketched over the writing to see if he could tell what the last thing was, she wrote on the pad. A number appears within the sketch. It is an inhouse number area code that is the same as Romania; someone is helping her. They placed the call to try to find Tracy, but the call was not able to go through.

"I wouldn't be surprised if it's a burned phone. No need to place another call, Casey. Don't waste your time."

The phone rang. It was Istvan with information for Chase.

{"I am calling notifying you that Tracy Fletcher has been found. Her friend got her to a city called Pitesti Romania. I will send you the address to her location."}

Chase received the address to her location. They had a 4-hour drive ahead of them. Istvan found out that she was also given a job in a restaurant called Cornel Pub. They would get there in 500 hundred hours. When they arrived at her location, they rented a car. They drove down the road and up to the area park. They walk up from behind her place. Tracy did not even know what hit her. She was startled. She starts running out the back door to her car. Casey retrieves her from behind. She raises her feet to a full blow and places it right on top of his feet so hard that Casey began to scream like a little Bitch. She turns around, grabs his arm, and does a Kata Seoi Nage move. Casey went over her head and fell to the ground. He was caught totally off guard by the move she performed. In the middle of all that, Chase walks outside and fires his gun. A piece falls from off the top of the shelter, hits Tracy's car, and busts out the front window. She turns around and looks at Casey.

89

"Omg...it's you. What are you both doing here?"

"You are acting surprised..."

He gets up slowly, grunting from the pain of being thrown around like a rag doll.

"Neither of you didn't care to get back in touch about the witness program, so I left. When people find out about this Black Book my brother kept a secret, people will be coming after me for this book."

The Colombian Cartels got an inkling of Chase and Casey being in Romania. They are looking for revenge on the ass whipping they received from them the last time Chase and Casey was there so they did not need to be in one place for too long.

BOOOOM!!

The car they parked down the road had blown up. Casey, Chase and Tracy duck down. A truck full of men pulls up.

Leader of the gang (yelling): *"YOU ALL ARE BACK. THIS TIME, I'M GOING TO GIVE YOU AN ASS WHIPPING"*

Tracy, Casey, and Chase look back and notice it was the Colombian Cartel hunch men.

"How did they know we were here?"

"Guys, this town is very small. We can head to the woods to get out of here. It is a long walk, but we must make a move or we will not survive."

They both check their weapons. They only had two magazines left and one in the firearm.

Casey (looks at Chase): *"What's the plan?"*

"Why is it always me coming up with a plan?"

"Let's try and make it across the field towards the woods."

Tracy falls, and when she gets up, she is limping but she takes off running. The leader of the gang saw them running across the field. They drove over humps and around trees trying to get there before they made it into the woods. Just before they made it, one of the henchmen jumps off the jeep, leaps over, and falls on Casey. They both went tumbling down into the ditch inside the wooded area. As Casey jumps up, he seems to have broken his neck. Casey ran behind Chase and Tracy through the woods.

Leader of the gang (yelling out): *"I'LL FIND YOU!"*

"Wooded areas have no reception. We are setting ducks out here. Casey how you are holding "Never better. We need to find our way out before all hell breaks loose."

"...If we haven't reached hell yet!"

The leader and his men jump out the jeep heading into the wooded area and split up in three's.

"Chase, they are not going to give up. We need a plan. We passed a community about 30 miles ahead of us. Maybe we can get word to Miller about getting some help."

"It will be too late. It's too many of them. We do not have enough ammo to hold them off."

"Think Chase, Think... ok!"

"Let's keep moving because sitting here is not a good idea. They are not too far behind us. Casey, I will go back track taking them out one by one. I will catch up to you both before you reach that community up ahead."

"Sounds like a plan."

Chase walks back. As he starts getting closer to where he thought they would be coming from, he climbs up a tree and waits for the last one to pass by. He jumped down and held him in a choke hold. He left the other two by themselves. He went out to find the other guys. As the dark started to creep in, they could barely see three feet in front of them. Chase ran up in front of them and the fight began. Chase took his knife and threw it at the first guy. It lands right in the middle of his chest. He fell to the ground quickly. The other two almost trip over him. Shots were being fired and Chase ducked down. Immediately Chase pulls out his 45 calibers with a laser for an easier target. Two rounds went out and hit its intended target. They both lay flat out with no signs of life.

Casey heard a noise from a gun. He and Tracy both stop and look at each other. Tracy was wondering what had just happened. They began running faster trying to get from that area. The noise of the gun going off was not too far behind them. Chase went back for the other two he left. This time he was not planning on leaving anyone behind. Chase ran so fast until it seemed like he was running a marathon. As he came up to the two, he whistled. They turn around. He knocks out one with a deadly kick to the head and the other with a blow to his chest. Now the leader and the rest of his folks are somewhere close by. The leader heard the fire of the gun going off. He warned his men to be on their P'S and Q'S. As the night darkens, the air gets cooler, along with a hint of quietness, the leader stops. He heard someone, or something, running through the woods.

Leader (to his men): *"Quiet, stop!"*

Before he knew it, he heard the whistling of a knife hollowing through the wind. The leader ducks but one of his men takes a knife to his esophagus. The other one starts running. The leader turns around and shoots him in the back. Now it is just Chase and the leader. Chase walks up to the leader, quickly provoking him.

"I knew you all were dirty, but to shoot your man in his back.... that doesn't come as a surprise. I guess that's just the way you handle business."

Within a split second, Chase turns around and kicks the gun out of his hand. The leader jab punches Chase to the face, but he shakes it off. Chase turns around, takes his thumb, and whips the blood off that was on the corner of his mouth. He then gets into a position for hand-to-hand combat. He was trained well, and he wanted to exhibit what he learned over the years, so he suckers punched him in his ribs. The leader returns a sidekick to Chase's chest, knocking the wind out of him with a devastating blow. It stuns Chase and pushes him back a few feet. Chase got his bearings and answers with an uppercut. The move gave the leader his final blow to the temple. He knew precisely to deliver the blow straight to his head. The leader fell dead. Chase was damn nearly out of breath. He needed to make it before Casey made that phone call to Miller. He was running through the woods trying to make it before Casey got there. He was running with everything he had, dashing through the woods, trying to get there. At times, he felt like he was not going to make it. The bitter night had given his eyesight an impaired judgement. He lucks up and sees an older man with a horse and buggy. He hopes on the older man's ride. Chase made it to the rendezvous just in time. All three arrived at the same time.

Casey (looks at Chase): *"You made it!"*

They both gave each other a high-5. Pulling up at a gas station, they made the call. Miller picks up the phone.

Casey: *"Sir, we are ready for air lift. We did run into a little trouble, but we are safe. We are in the România location Pitesti Romania."*

{"Sending air lift out. I have your coordinates. Welcome back Chase. Thanks Casey. Smooth sailing from here on out."}

There was a sandy dark road ahead of them and they looked around and noticed a cloud of dust kicking up. As the vehicle headed towards them fast, they took cover behind an old, abandoned vehicle. The one that got away earlier went back to get reinforcements. The jeep halts to a stop. When they look around, they see the man that Chase allowed to get away. He jumps outside the jeep to look around.

Chase (whispers): *"Dammit!"*

"Now what?"

"That is the same idiot that I let get away. Common sense should have told him to keep running. I guess he has not learned his lesson yet to know when just to walk away."

"Chase, I have rested up enough. I am in a good mood to kick some Colombian ass tonight."

Casey comes out of hiding.

Chase (whispers): *"Casey, come back!"*

Casey walks up halfway to the man.

"May I help you?"

The man takes one look at Casey and recognizes him. He then points his figure at Casey while looking back towards the jeep. He was letting his guys know, in his language, that Casey is one of them. Casey knew he was recognized. He figured this was it, so what the hell. Casey ran up and did a double kick and he knocked the guy straight back towards the jeep to the ground.

"Tracy, stay put. I'm going out there with Casey!"

"Casey, you were not planning on taking all the credit for this were you?"

"I might be a little older than you, but I still have a few tricks up my sleeves."

A total of five men surrounded them. Before the bad men realize, Chase grabs one of them by his throat, pushing him away in a violent movement. He then sucker punches him to the temple. He collapses to the ground. Casey shifts his feet back and moves with a high kick in the air that is so powerful until it pushes the man back far. He stumbles just before he falls to the ground. Casey came at him with deadly force and the other two men backed up. From a distance, they both look at Casey with fire and rage in their eyes. After taking out three men, there were two men left standing. Each man stands face to face and they begin to square off. Chase reaches down into his boot and pulls his combat knife out. He stands, leaning back, dodging the man's fearless blows. Chase moves forward, he ducks and dodges the man next hit. Chase knees him to his lower abdomen. The man bends forward from the pain in the stomach. Chase grabs the man's right arm and twists it around to where his opponent arm snaps. Chase opponents were forces to be reckoned with. They were standing straight with a slight lean bending backward. Chase uses his left hand to wield his combat knife. He begins slashing his opponent's main arteries from his wrist. He then moves up to the side of the man's neck, slicing his vein. He lets his opponent go as he hemorrhages out from his injuries. Meanwhile, Casey uses a wrestling move on his opponent. He pins his opponent in a position to where he could not free himself. Casey then shifts his body weight, and his opponent was in a locked position and was not able to move. Casey breaks his arm then Chase shoots Casey's opponent in the chest as Casey releases him and he falls to his death.

"I had him!"

"You took too long."

It was over. They were all deceased. Chase and Casey heard a helicopter flying. Tracy comes out of hiding. A IAR 330 Puma Romanian Air force was hovering over them. Their ride came in the middle of the eerie night. There was a steam of smoke rising from their breath on a cold freezing night. The IAR 330 came so close until it lighted up the night sky. All three turn their heads as it lands in the middle of the road. They wanted to hurry and get on board to keep the sand from getting their eyes. They jump on the aircraft. Miller was sitting comfortably on board. Everyone was startled.

"Sir, I see you are here as well."

"What...you don't think I need to be in the field? I was out in the field before you even thought about joining the CIA. (looks at Tracy) Here are your papers."

Tracy (happy): *"Thank you, Sir!"*

"Tracy, I wish you would've just talked to me. I thought you and I had a better understanding..."

"I am deeply sorry, Sir. I just did not know who I could trust."

Miller (talking to them all): *"We are being taken to Bucharest; the Capital of Romania. From there, we have a Gulfstream G500 waiting."*

"Mr. Miller, Sir, what is our mission on Dimitri Petrov on getting him back to the US?"

"Dimitri Petrov's mission will consist of you bringing him back to America alive. I believe we have substantial evidence for his case."

"We have the evidence. Now, all we need is to bring him in for the crimes that he has committed."

"We have to plan this right. The Attorney General and I were working together on trying to get Dimitri on war crimes against foreign policies and smuggling, but there will be complications in trying to pursue this avenue."

Chase and Casey (responding at Miller simultaneously): "COMPLICATIONS?"

"Both of you, I am here because I have some bad news. Dimitri's father has powerful connections. His ties to Russia are well connected, so we cannot get the Immunity waived. We will need to go over the evidence to see if it is strong enough to bring him in that way."

They made it in the Capital of Romania to the US Embassy. They walked towards the gate, and inside, they were welcomed by Ambassador Nel Finch. They walk toward the back getting Tracy's papers ready for witness protection from the United States Department of Justice.

Ambassador: (speaking with Miller): "When you step foot inside the United States, the US Marshals will be standing by for Mrs. Tracy Fletcher. They will then take Mrs. Tracy Fletcher to her new life."

Tracy was handed her papers as she gave them her brother's little black book.

Tracy (walking up to Chase): "Thank you for getting my papers and for saving my life back in Pitesti."

Miller (stepping aside talking with the Ambassador): *"We are in a hurry Ambassador. Would you be able to get us a ride out of there to the airfield? I have a plane standing by waiting for us."*

"No Problem!" (he walks off)

"Guys, you will be debriefed in the next hour."

Chase (walks up to Miller): *"What did Dimitri do that made the Colombian Cartels run after him? The Head of the Colombian Cartel was supposed to supply Dimitri with Drugs. Dimitri was going to give them the explosives for a tread payment for the drugs, but instead, Dimitri took back the explosives including the drugs. Dammit, he never gave them back the drugs he stole. When we came in to take Dimitri, we didn't make it any better…matter of fact, we made them a hell of a lot angrier."*

"WHAT!"

"Yeah, when we picked up Dimitri from Budapest, they were in the country also and we had a run-in with the Colombians. I guess we hurt their pride, so now they are looking for revenge because we took Dimitri away from them. We also shorten their gang. The Head Colombian Cartel in charge of these men is sending him out on a blood bath."

Right outside the Embassy, they heard a big explosion right by the door of the gate. The guard outside the door rushes inside after locking down the gate making sure no one comes through the door of the Embassy.

"What was that?"

"It is the Extraction team letting us know they are watching us. What's the plan guys?"

"Make sure all the windows and doors are locked up tight so no one could get in."

Ambassador (comes rushing back): *"We have someone coming in to pick you all up in 20 min.!"*

A few seconds later, they hear fighter jets roaring multiple times from the Romanian Air Force. Streets are cleared. Thirty minutes later, a military armored vehicle, along with two military Humvee (JLTV) comes up.

Captain (walking in): *"Someone needs a lift?"*

Miller walks up and shakes the captain's hand. The captain addresses Miller as "Sir". Miller pulls the captain away for a talk. They came back with bulletproof vests. Tracy, Casey, Chase, and Miller gear up getting ready to pull out. They walk outside the Embassy. The streets are clear. They approach the armored vehicle, and they get in. The captain rides up front getting them to the airfield safely. The G500 sits there on stand-by. They all sigh with relief. Miller again approaches the captain with a salute along with a hand shake. Miller pats the captain's back with gratitude. Miller smiles and runs to the plane. They all get settled in for takeoff. Their mission is completed. Tracy's mission was an almost success.

Pilot (comes over the intercom): {"Sir, I'm glad to see your mission was successful. Relax because we came well prepared. Set back and enjoy your flight home. The weather is beautiful. We estimated your arrival time 15 hours from now."}

They all rest up before landing. After a couple hours of sleep, they woke up to refreshments, a lite sandwich, and a beverage. They talk about getting Dimitri out of Russia as they conclude everything.

Casey got up and walked around exercising his legs. He strolls over to Tracy and takes a seat.

"Tracy, we were able to locate your brother's body and gave him a proper burial. Wherever your new location will be, your brother's plot will remain well maintained."

Tracy (shakes his hands): *"Thank you!"*

Chase (walks over to them): *"You both are really in a deep conversation over here."*

"Chase, that is between Tracy and me."

Casey then gets up and walks off. Tracy smiles at Chase.

Pilot: (comes over the intercom): {"Welcome to Virginia. The temperature is 26 degrees with a 10% chance of rain in the forecast today. Please stay seated. Estimated arrival time now is 30 minutes."}

Miller (walks over towards Tracy): *"That the US Marshals are standing by. (Miller hugs Tracy) It has been a pleasure. Take care."*

Chase and Casey smiled as they all properly stayed seated buckled in, the plane started to land. The plane lands at the Private hangar area away from commercial aircrafts. As they disembark the plane, the US Marshals Walk up and approach Miller as they flash their badge. Miller escorted the marshals over to Tracy.

Miller: *"Tracy Fletcher, this is the US Marshal. You will be heading in with them for the witness protection program."*

"Will I be seeing any of you again?"

"You bet, when the trail starts."

US Marshals escort Tracy towards the SUV. The engine starts up. The door closes and the SUV starts to leave the area. Moments later, two more US marshals walked through the door and were heading straight towards Miller. Chase and Casey eye the two federal agents as they introduce themselves. Casey reads their vest. US Marshal.

"Our witness just left with your men 10 minutes ago."

US Marshal 1: *"Can't be...We were the only ones who knew about this assignment."*

US Marshal 2 (calls in for a search of the vehicle description that was given to them by Miller): *"We are looking for a black SUV that will have 2 men and 1 female. The men will be dressed like agents."*

US Marshal 1 (calls the office to get information): *"Were there any other US Marshals involved on our assignment?"*

Voice from phone: {*"Negative sir, you both were assigned to that duty per Attorney General."*}

"Dammit...they took her."

Chase and Casey jumps in a car taking off after the phony US Marshals. After driving for a few moments, Casey drives and pulls up behind them full throttle. The phony US Marshalls looks in the mirror and begins accelerating faster. Chase was in full pursuit.

Miller (making a call to the local policemen): {*"Please be alerted that Secret Service Agents are out on a car chase. DO NOT ENGAGE. I repeat...DO NOT ENGAGE!"*}

Tracy (looks puzzled): *"Hey guys, I think they want you to pull over."*

They both ignore Tracy and foot the gas a bit more. Tracy starts to panic. She hops up trying to grab the steering wheel. They grab her face and shove her down with a force. She pushes herself up in the seat looking dismantled. She looks back and notices it is Casey and Chase. She then realizes that they are not the real US Marshals. Tracy starts thinking and wondering why they kidnapped her because she could not possibly have anything they could want. As she is fully upward in the seat, she leans over towards the passenger and grabs his neck in a choke-hold. The driver looks over and hits her with the butt of his gun across the left side of her temple. He let her know, in no uncertain terms, that if she doesn't sit back in the seat that he will shoot her in the leg. She took one look at him and headbutted the phony Marshal on the passenger side in the head to make sure he was out. Then she leaned towards the driver and bit down on his ear so hard that she took a chunk of his ear off. He bent over in the seat holding his ear. The car swerves so the other Marshal grabs a hold of the steering wheel. In contrast, the driver screams in pain as she continues biting down on his ear. She methodically plunges back in her seat gunning for the car door.

Phony Marshall-Passenger (pulls her hair bringing her back inside the SUV): *"Be still if you know what was good for you."*

Phony Marshal-Driver (screaming): *"She just bit my Fu**** ear, OMG! my Fu**** ear.* (He looks over at the other guy with his figure tips tapping his ear) *Did she just takes a chunk off?"*

Phony Marshall-Passenger (reassuring him): *"It isn't bad.* (looks back at Tracy) *You better be lucky they want you alive."*

Chase and Casey drive on the side of them, trying to run them off the road. The phony marshals deviate to keep them from running into them. A truck comes piling down the road in the same direction Chase and Casey are. Caseys in the driver seat.

Chase (yelling): *"CASEY, WATCH OUT FOR THE TRUCK!"*

Casey veers off and just misses the truck by the skim of his pants. He swerved into a ditch and lost them. They both climb out of the car.

"DAMMIT, WHAT NOW?"

Chase (holds his head down): *"We need to call Miller."*

Miller (on phone): {"Who would want to kidnap her, who has something to lose?"}

Miller sent a car out to pick them up and they headed back to headquarters. They walk in the office to find Miller on the phone. Casey and Chase walked in waiting for Miller to finish his phone conversation. Miller calmly sets the receiver down.

"Chase and Casey, the agency, feels like Blaze is responsible for Tracy's kidnapping. He's in court right now as we speak. He is facing 25 years in Federal prison. The little black book is evidence for him going even much longer in prison."

"We need to find Tracy!"

"By the time we get ready to pick up Dimitri, it will be five years from now. Something is always holding us back. I cannot emphasize strongly enough that he needs to answer for these crimes he committed."

Miller (to them both): *"He should get punished. You both need to report back here. (the phone rings) It is Department of Defense (DOD) Chase, they did not say a name, but its your wife."*

Casey hears Miller tell Chase that it is his wife on the other end of the phone. It was a five minute phone call.

Chase (turns around): *"Mr. Miller, Sir the Pentagon called me. I will meet up with you all tomorrow."* (Chase leaves out.)

Casey (catches up with him): *"Why did you never tell me that you're married?"*

"I didn't think I needed to tell you I was."

"Aren't we partners? I thought we are supposed to know everything about each other if this partner-relationship is going to work."

"Casey; we will talk about this tomorrow. Now if you'll excuse me I have somewhere I need to be!"

Chase walks off and gets in his vehicle. As he drives off, he calls his wife. Riley, the next door neighbor, answers the phone.

"Do you need me?"

{"Yeah, one of my officers ran into 2 Marshals at the hospital. One got a chunk of his ear bit off."}

"Those are our guys."

{"I kind of figured it out. They had a female with them. She looked pretty shaken up. She also left a letter in the restroom. One of the nurses found it and gave it to her husband; one of our officers. They could not hold the US Marshal, but they did gave him a prescription to get filled."}

"Thanks. Tell Alexa I will be home later."

Chase hangs up and damn near tears a hole in the floor of his car from pressing the gas pedal so hard. He gets to the store not too far from the hospital and he calls it in. The office caught Casey and Miller just in time.

{"Chase, wait until we get there. Do not engage."}

Miller and Casey run out the door into the car garage. Casey got in the driver seat.

"Casey, I heard about your driving. There is not going to be any of that here right?"

"Oh yes Sir."

Casey's mind went blank and numb as he halls ass leaving Miller damn near in a panic and holding on to dear life. They finally made it to the store in fifteen minutes on a thirty minute drive. They walk right into gunfire with bullets flying everywhere and Chase ducking and dodging bullets.

"Chase, I will handle you later. You disregard everything I told you to do. I gave you an order to "DO NOT ENGAGE" and you went and did the total opposite."

The phony Marshal grabs Tracy and shoves her to the floor while bullets are flying. Casey takes one look at where one of the sham Marshals was standing and shoots a plastic soda bottle. It sprays directly in his face. He starts blocking his face trying to keeping the soda from his eyes. Tracy tries to get up on her feet but the other Marshall grabs her and shoves her down to the floor. She was crawling on the floor while gasping for air. Casey looks over at Tracy and he knew she was in immense pain. He resolved that Tracy must have given them a hell of a fight.

Miller (yelling from where he is standing): *"CHASE!"*

He signals sign language telling him to box them into where they cannot leave the store. Chase starts boxing them in. The other guy catches on to what they were trying to do. He takes a shot at Chase, trying to keep him from boxing them in. One of the Marshals picks up Tracy by her shirt and starts dragging her through the store. As he drags her, he starts thinking to himself that because she bit a piece of his ear off, that she needs to pay. He continues dragging her through the store. Tracy spots some lighter fluid and places her leg on the shelf knocking them down. She was able to grab a bottle of the fluid. The Marshal was so angry, and into his thoughts about destroying her, until he did not even notice what she did. He stops and picks her up off the floor. By then, she was able to open the bottle of lighter fluid, and without delay, she sprays his eyes. She gets him so good that he had no choice except to scream at the top of his lungs and he falls to the floor. The other marshal runs over, picks him up, and places his hand on his shoulders. The sham marshal 1 snatches Tracy off the floor. He pulls out a bazooka, points it at the microwave, and fires; it explodes with dangerous sparks. Chase, Miller, and Casey duck down to the concrete floor. The marshals, along with Tracy, run out the door. Before pulling out of the parking lot, they shoot out the tires of the other two unmarked government vehicles.

CHAPTER FIVE

Finding Tracy Fletcher

LOCAL COPS WERE dispatched out on the scene. Riley walks up as Chase is getting his ass chewed out for disobeying Miller's instructions. Casey stands there eyeing everyone.

Riley (walks up to Casey): *"What is going on?"*

"Chase violated a direct order."

Riley (walks away and goes over to Miller): *"Miller, the CIA has jurisdiction over this. We will do some leg work then after that, we will hand the case over to you all.*

Miller (shakes Riley's hand): *"Sounds good!"* (walks off)

Riley (walks over to Chase): *"I will catch up with you later."*

Miller, Casey, and Chase walk into the store. They talk to the store manager then they walk in his office demanding the security footage to the store. They need to view it. Hopefully they can get something useful out of it.

Casey (walks over to Chase): *"Why did you feel like you could not wait?"*

Chase: *"I felt like we let Tracy down. I felt like we didn't try hard enough in protecting her."* Casey: *"That might be, but you disobey direct orders on not engaging until we got here so you would have back-up."*

Miller leaves the two men talking and walks outside. The Administration wrecker pulls up getting both Government Vehicles after dropping off transportation for them. Casey walks up to the driver door.

Miller (walks over towards Casey): *"I will drive. We have had enough of your driving tonight Casey."*

A call came in for Miller.

Voice: {"You all are needed back at the office."}

Miller (glancing over at Chase with a smirk): *"I'm not finished with you yet for your actions."*

They made it to the office and the US Department of Justice was in the office waiting for them. Someone reached out wanting the little black book that Tracy was thought to have. They waited for the return phone call, and two hours later, the call came in.

Voice: {"The meeting place will take place in Fairfax Virginia by the Potomac River around 1600 hours and bring the black book!"}

The request was not traceable because it ended too quickly.

US Department of Justice: *"Now we wait. Everyone meets here in the morning at 1100 hundred hours."*

Casey: *"Today was a long exhausting day. We came back from Romania to this mess. (walking out) I will see everyone tomorrow morning."*

Meanwhile, they were holding Tracy captive in a basement with an old damp, wet mildew smell. She hears the two men that kidnapped her talking to someone on the phone.

{"The meeting will be taking place at 1600 hundred hours. Be there by 1500 hundred hours and try do not be late!"}

She hears them talking about the black book and that Blaze will be there tomorrow with their money. Tracy starts murmuring to herself that Blaze is behind all of this. One of the pretend marshals comes in and unties her hands to eat. The next morning, Blaze stops by to check his merchandise out. He walks into the room and begins asking her questions about the black book her brother kept up until his death.

"Did you read the book?"

"Why you ask? Even if I did read the book, I would never tell you?"

"Does the book have anything about me in it?"

"Blaze, would it matter? You already added kidnapping to your charges."

"So, you're refusing to tell me anything?"

"You would find out in court. I am quite sure they are going to lock you up in Federal Prison. Do you know what they do to people in prison? You should have been like your rivalry instead of venturing out into the big league. You should have stayed in the little league. You are most definitely going to pay just like your blood brother Dimitri. He killed my brother, and you are an accessory of it all. You are going to do as much time as he does. I can't wait for that judgment day. Stop asking me questions and worry about yourself."

"What you are jabbering about is neither here nor there. I am trading you for the book."

Tracy starts squirming in her seat trying to get free. In her mind, her brother would have died in vain if they were to give the book to Blaze.

Meanwhile, back at headquarters. Miller is getting ready for the drop off, not sure what the plan is. He is certain that the government does not negotiate with terrorists. The plan has to be cunning. Miller is in the office. He is trying to find some options on what is going to take place. Everyone is thinking too much. Casey needs to clear his head. He is getting ready to turn over evidence that could put away Dimitri and Blaze for a very long time. He also knew the government was not going to give them that book. Casey realizes he needs to come up with a plan, so he goes out and does his usual method to take his mind off things; he went out for a jog. After his 5-mile jog, he walks up the steps drenched in sweat. He spots a glare from off the windowpane of the apartment building. He could see a black, tinted-window SUV barreling down the street. Someone rolls down the window and places a Bazooka halfway out secured against his shoulder. Casey dove over the balcony in the wild bushes. The Bazooka launched and caused a massive hole in the front of the building. The hole was big enough to drive a car through. It shook up the whole neighborhood with car alarms going off and dogs barking in the background. Casey gradually sets up, looking around, hoping that the car kept going. His phone rings and he realize it is Miller on the other end of the phone

Casey (answers): *"Sir!"*

{"Casey, are you okay? A call just came through on a red alert for your neighborhood. I am on the way. Chase is dispatched out."}

"I'm ok. My ego is a little bruised, but I am fine."

A few minutes later, Miller and Chase pull up. They ran up to the building to see the vast hole. Riley and the whole local police department, Fire Departments, and Paramedics were all on the scene. They were coming in and out of the apartment building rescuing people. Chase, Casey, and Miller were talking among themselves.

Casey (talking to Miller): *"It was the phony Marshals. They used a bazooka."*

"This is getting very serious."

All three got in the car heading back to the office. The Department of Justice worked on this mission all night long. They all are wondering the same thing. They were able to pose as US Marshals so they had access to the proper uniforms. There has to be a leak somewhere. No one knew about the task but that department.

The Deputy Director comes into the office.

Miller (walks up and shakes his hand): *"Looks like we have something on our hands."*

Deputy Director: *"Miller, would you like to accompany me back to my office? Chase and Casey, I am going to need your help as well."*

Miller (answering for them all): *"It will be our honor!"*

As they arrived in Washington, DC, they went directly to the Department Of Justice building walking straight into the interrogation room. A middle-aged US Marshal agent is sitting in a chair. The Deputy Director, Miller, Chase, and Casey were looking in the room through a door.

The Director (speaking to Chase, Casey, and Miller): *"We have a leak. His name is Boidi. He is the one who leaked it out about Tracy Fletcher being accepted for the witness protection program and that she has some evidence of Blaze and Dimitri."*

"I need to talk with this agent!" (walking in with Casey)

"Miller, I am a part of this team, and I need to be in there as well while you all are interrogating him."

"You are most definitely on my shit list for disobeying direct orders."

Casey looks over towards Chase and shrugs his shoulders as he walks into the interrogation room. The Deputy Director and Chase looked in on them both while they were interviewing the agent.

Miller (starts off talking to the agent): *"Looks like you are in a world of mess. Would you like to volunteer in telling us why you leaked this information out?"*

Boidi: *"You must promise me that you will protect my family and me."*

Miller: *"It depends on what type of information you can give us."*

Boidi: *"Blaze hired someone to pose as a driver. They came to my home and took my family. They are holding them hostage. He also threatened me that if I don't cooperate, he would kill my family. I did what he wanted. They told me my family would return to me after they received the black book. I can't go home until my shift is over because they are watching my home. If I leave abruptly, they are going to know that I was caught and released from duties."*

Miller and Casey agree that he has a point. They walk out discussing their options of what is next with Chase and the Deputy Director of DOJ. While they were talking with the agent, the Deputy Director and Chase formed an idea. They thought they could rewrite their own 'little black book' just enough to pass for a trade of Tracy Fletcher. The plan sounds good and doable, but they wondered about Boidi. They figured he would more than likely get reprimanded with no jail time since he was trying to keep his family alive. If he continues to cooperate, he will be fine. It was now 1300 hours, and with three hours to go, they needed to leave. It will take them about two hours from there to get to the location. They stop by Langley to gather up the troops. The plans are set into motion.

Temporarily, Blaze and his men are ready, waiting, and geared up for a war. They untie Tracy and take the blindfold off. In her mind, something was not right. Tracy knew that once she could identify her kidnappers, there was no way in hell they were going to let her go. She starts to panic and looks for a way out if or when she would be able to run. Time was of the essence. She did the only thing she could think of; she fainted. They ran over towards her. Blaze takes one look at her and tells them to pick her up and put her in the van. She knew she had to get away before they got to where they were going to take her. Blaze and the phony US Marshal rode together while Tracy was in a black tinted window van. There were two vans; the first was full of Blaze men; the second van was with a driver, passenger, and Tracy. The second followed Blaze and the phony federal marshals as they were heading south out of town.

Meanwhile, Miller, Deputy Director, Chase, and Casey had no time, so they hired a forger to write another copy of the black book but with false information about Blaze and Dimitri affairs. They knew just about everything when it came to Blaze and Dimitri, along with their tactic plans they both had together. The twist was only to half fill it. The killing that took place will not get placed in the book. Chase was the sniper within 2000 yards away from the drop off with an M82 Sniper rifle. He climbed high as he could, looking down on them with a clearer shot. All the other agents were scattered everywhere having the best unobstructed view they could find.

They arrive at the location 1500 hours, just a little shy of 5 minutes before the phony marshals did. The van that held Tracy hostage was sitting just outside of Virginia, heading on 26 south. The two vans separated enroute. Everyone had on their earpiece so they would all be able to stay in contact with one another. Blaze is nowhere to be seen. He was dropped off somewhere before they arrived.

Casey (runs over towards Miller): *"Blaze is not in the car."*

"We would worry about him when the time comes. We have more pressing business at hand."

As they pull up, one of the phony marshals gets out of the car.

Casey (walks over towards him): *"We need to see Tracy Fletcher."*

"Not before I see the black book."

"You have misunderstood. There is NO negotiation. NO Tracy Fletcher; NO black book."

Chase hears the whole conversation. He scans the perimeter and spots the black van with tinted windows placed not too far away from the drop-off. Shortly thereafter, he sees men climbing out of the vehicle fully loaded with weapons. Chase comes over the earpiece

"Casey. You all have company from the east of you coming up fast. The men are narrowing down the perimeter and securing the area, closing in on you, Miller, and two other agents."

Phony Marshal (demanding Casey): *"If I don't get the black book, I will not have a problem killing the woman."*

Chase hears the conversation, as he takes one look at the area through his sniper sight viewer. He has the Phony Marshal in range. Miller's hand goes down and Chase takes the shot. The Phony Marshal takes a hit to the chest and goes down. The other phony marshal puts the car in reverse and backs into a tree. Chase flattens the tire on the van. not too far from the drop off point. Two men come behind Miller and Casey. Miller turns around and punches him in the throat with the butt of his gun. While the other man clutches Casey by his shoulders, Casey takes his wrist and flips him over his shoulder. The man went tumbling down into the water. Casey drags him out by his broken wrist onto dry land.

Casey: (asking the man while his feet are on his chest): *"Where is she? Where is Tracy Fletcher? I will only ask you once."*

The man looks at Casey with a deadly stare. Casey bent and stood over him looking him in his eyes. He knew he was not going to get any information out of him. Casey then knocks him out with one strike to the face.

Casey (gets on his earpiece): *"Chase, are there anymore?"*

{"Five more coming up the rear side of you"}

Casey ran and hid by the car one of the men passed by. He runs and does a high kick with both feet put together in the air and knocks him down. The man tumbled hard to the ground. Casey gets up and sidekicks the man. The man then grabs hold of Casey's foot; not letting go. Casey does another kick with his right leg into the air and the man goes down.

Casey (comes up from behind and whispers in his ear): *"You should have told me where she is. Now, you are about to pay!"*

Casey puts him in a chokehold. The man struggles to break free. Casey presses down even harder to gain full control. He then snaps the man's neck to the right. Just one snap from the pressure and the man had no life in him. Casey walks off with disbelief and out of breath.

Casey (talks through his earpiece): *"Miller, Sir. We have three more."*

Miller was already engaged with one of them so that left two. Both men came running from behind a boulder. Chase had his eyes on both. One went down from a bullet wound straight to his chest. The other one came at Casey with a machete. Casey ran straight, leaped up in the air into the boulder, lifted his right leg, and kicked the back of the man's head. The man shakes off the blow that was decently delivered. He charges back for more. The man takes a swing with the machete. Casey bent backward, slid his feet straight out toward the man, and the machete fell to the ground. He lands with a hard blow.

Casey (over his earpiece): "I don't think she is here you guys.

{"I believe you are right!"}

They all come together. Miller got on the phone with the Department of Justice. Miller relays the message to the agents.

They spotted a van heading south on 26 interstates. Blaze's arrested from his estate; they caught him packing and burning his documents. They arrested Blaze on the charges of smuggling, warfare, treason, and murder. Blaze could get massive jail time.

"Miller, did they find Tracy yet?

"They caught up with the van on interstate 26 swerving. The local police pulled them over. One of the guys had a black eye while the driver had a piece of his ear missing. Tracy is exceptional. They are bringing them all back in for questioning."

The cleanup crew arrived along with more agents on the scene. The Deputy Director also made it through. They all went back to the office to deal with questioning Blaze and his men.

Deputy Director: *"Do you all know why or how he got out the last time? He was a NO flight risk then. That has since changed. His bail was set at 2.5 million, this time he is behind bars until his court date."*

They were walking through the building by the time they arrived. The US Marshals had already taken Tracy. She gave her statement then they rushed her out immediately. Miller, Casey, nor Chase got to see her. Casey thought to himself that the important thing to remember is that she is safe. The US Marshals come in along with the Department of State and Deputy directly escorting Blaze out.

"Both of you take tomorrow off!"

Casey (walking out with chase and a little disappointed): *"I wonder why she did not try to say anything to us?"*

"We will see her again when the court date comes. Besides, it was not her choice not to say anything to us. They were rushing her out!"

"I guess you are right. She would have talked to her if it were up to her!"

Miller (speaks to them as they walk out for the day): *"Job well done you guys."*

Casey (walking side by side): *"Chase, are we not friends?"*

"Yes, we are. I know what's going through your mind. Our first mission together is going to take some time, but just know this; I will always have your back."

Casey (turning around): *"That made my day. Dido."*

With everything that has transpired, Casey thought he would stop by to see Bella. Casey knocks on the door as he enters her home.

Casey (excited): *"Ma."*

Bella (walks out of the room): *"Son, long time no see."*

"Mother, I have been busy. How have you been?"

"Son, horrible... Due to current circumstances, my client has been arrested again by violating his bail condition. This time I don't think I will be able to get him out under these conditions."

"Can you even tell me who he is?"

"Nope, that is confidentiality. I am not at liberty to discuss this case whatsoever. I kind of feel sorry for him, but he caused this himself. I must see him tomorrow. He needs my help. Being honest though, there isn't anything I can do but take a plea bargain. He's not going to like it."

"Ma, I just wanted to put my eyes on you to make sure you're okay. We will talk later. Maybe we can meet somewhere for dinner. I might be out of the country in a few weeks. My job is sending me on a film shot learning about stage cameras."

Casey kisses his mother and walks out the door.

Casey arrives home feeling lost. His mind is on Dimitri and a curtain destination, RUSSIA! Casey murmurs to himself that he will not rest until Dimitri is put away for good. He needs to gradually take his mind off the mission and focus on something different. He heads to his bedroom and slides off his rugged jeans. As Casey puts on his biker shorts with his silky-smooth thin young body, he begins his night meditating. He then heads to the gym on his 5-mile jog with his earpiece listening to music clearing his mind and discerning his thoughts from Dimitri. Casey walks into the gym for a full-fledged workout. Afterwards, he runs back to his apartment sweating on the cold night. Casey walks into his apartment and gaits toward his bathroom with sweat pouring down his face. He looks up, towards the mirror, gazing at his face posing and flexing in the mirror. He knew that he needed to get his mind off Dimitri but once again he started to wonder what it would take to capture him. He starts feeling a sting in the back of his leg from the extent of his workout and the lack of water intake. He slides into his shower, hoping the steam would relax his muscle spasms. He got out of the shower and began getting ready for bed. Casey's phone rings. He answers on the second ring with a very sleepy hello. He heard heavy breathing without anyone answering, but he could hear someone breathing on the other end. After he hears the whispering of a deep breath, he hears a dial tone. His mind starts to wonder who the hell could that be. Strange things have been going on. Casey was becoming restless. He was so tired and then he began hearing his own heartbeat. The motion of his body was beginning to put him in a trance after hearing his heartbeat. Seconds later, he was out of sound sleep.

The next morning came like a bolt of lightning. It feels like the alarm went off too soon. Casey springs up like a well-rested rooster. His phone rings. It is Miller on the other end telling him that he is needed in the office immediately. Casey walks into the bathroom and looks at his slim face, masculine body, with his short boxed in beard, and his adorable sexy green eyes. Casey takes his shower and gets himself groomed and dressed; ready for his day to begin. He makes it to the building and walks from out of the garage heading in. He bumps into Chase and they both rush in together. Miller and the Attorney General are waiting for them.

"Guys; we are not able to get Dimitri in the way we were hoping. We have banned Dimitri from the US. If we could go back to Russia, kidnap Dimitri, and bring him back to the U.S., we can get him to enter the US without documentation. We could only keep him here for one to two-years max for entering the U.S. We can find a way by then to keep Dimitri here in the US in costumes for the crimes that he has committed."

Casey and Chase looked at each other and agreed. That evening they were getting ready for their trip back into Russia. They needed to plan their next move. The Attorney General made plans for Chase and Casey on the next flight out of Virginia after the weather cleared up a bit. Miller made the rest of the arrangements. That next morning, they are in debriefing with Miller and the Attorney General. Everything was ready. Making their way to the airfield, they knew they had no time to waste. As Casey and Chase make their way to Russia, they made a pact:

No man left behind!

CHAPTER SIX

Lost and Found

CHASE AND CASEY board the plane with nothing but Dimitri on their minds. Settling in, they fasten their seatbelts and prepare for departure from Virginia to Russia.

{"This is your Pilot speaking. Welcome aboard. I'm your pilot for today. We are departing Virginia heading to Russia. Our arrival time is approximately sixteen-hours. The current weather in Oblast Russia is 26 degrees Fahrenheit mixed with rain and snow. Relax and enjoy your ride. Have a good evening and an enjoyable flight."}

They settled in and prepared for the long flight. They did as the Pilot suggested and relaxed. They both had a little too much to drink and fell asleep in transit. Ten hours later, the flight attendant walked over to Casey.

Flight Attendant (handing Casey the phone): *"Sir, it's Langley, Mr. Miller."*

{"Casey, did you get a phone call the other night?"}

Before Casey could answer him, the plane started experiencing bad turbulence. Chase looked out the window. It looked like they got hit on the left side of the aircraft.

HELLO...HELLO MR. MILLER CAN YOU HEAR ME HELLO

The plane started losing altitude and was spiraling out of control. Casey grabbed the arm rest tightly, embedding his nails deep into the material. It slightly breaks in half. He did not know his own strength. In the cockpit the pilot said a plea for help.

WE HAVE TAKEN A HIT ON THE LEFT SIDE OF THE ENGINE COMPARTMENT. This is flight 00026. We are undergoing terrible turbulence. Our coordinates are 26*26 '02.6W. Come in..Come in.. This is flight 00026, 26*26'02.6W 26.

Seconds later static noise takes over the radio.

Casey was looking out of the small window from his seat. He sees the ocean a second later. They were over land. The plane is spiraling down this dark, dreaded wooded area. Night fell like a woven cloth covering the plane. They went down in some sort of jungle. Without spaces between the trees, it looked like nightfall, but it was still daytime. The dark starts to settle in the damp cold wooded area. The steam could be heard coming from the engine. Chase noticed smoke coming from the front of the plane. It is the cockpit. It burst into flames. Chase runs towards the cockpit, and using the fire extinguisher, was able to put out the flames. His heart is beating radically and his blood rushing flowing through his body. He looked over to see the pilot and co-pilot. Their bodies looked limped. He knew their lives were gone. The force from the plane broke the flight attendant's neck. That leaves Chase and Casey with no communication. They were miles away and no one could even see the smoke coming from the plane in a smoldering dark wooded area. Chase was becoming a lot more alert. He gets up to keep himself from being distressed, but he was feeling groggy and dismantled. Chase wakes up and looks over to Casey slumping over in his fastened seat. Chase crawls over towards Casey and checks for a pulse. He sighs with relief. Casey begins to awaken. Shaking his head from side to side, he gradually opens his eyes.

"How are you feeling?"

"I feel a little dizzy. What happened? All I saw was a lightning flash towards the left side of the plane and now here we are. Where exactly are we?"

"We can assume it is okay for you to have said all that in one breath."

"Where are we?"

"I heard you for the first time. How the hell am I supposed to know where we are?"

"Did you hear the pilot call out the coordinates while we were going down?"

Chase (sets there thinking with his eyes closed): *"I remember 26* um, um 26*26'02, um 02.6W, yeah 26* 26'02.6W."*

Well Chase, that means we should be somewhere in Ukraine. Where in Ukraine, I do not know."

"Well, that is close enough. We are going to assume that we are in YkpaiHa. We need to start packing a few things and move out before dark."

"I got a better idea...Why don't we start heading out early tomorrow morning. Seems as though we began our mission late so let us just stay put. Maybe back home they will begin to wonder. They should realize in another three hours we missed the ride to our destination. Can we both

agree tomorrow we start early? Let's get some wood for a fire; something tells me it gets cold here at night."

"Sounds like a plan and I'll go get some wood. You look around for food and maybe a blanket or two."

Casey found some food, a couple of quilts, and some cognac to keep there night warm. Chase walks back in where the plane crashed.

"You got everything we need?"

"Yes, and I found some flares to light up the campfire. Darks start to claim the day so we can start the campfire burning with flames. I found some MRE's in the back of the plane. I also buried the crew. We don't even know how long we are going to be here in this country."

"Before we began descending, you got a phone call from Miller. What did he want?"

"He never got to tell me what he wanted. He asked me did I get a phone call the night before we left. I never got the chance to answer."

"Well, did you get a phone call?"

"I did, but the person never said anything, just heavy breathing."

"That's just like you to get someone calling you breathing on the phone. Who did you piss off?"

"No one yet but let me find Dimitri. I'll have the whole syndicate being pissed at me."

Night was fully in, and it was difficult for them to see three feet in front of them. The next morning, Casey is up scooping around the perimeter. The noise from Casey stirring up wakes Chase. He had a little cough looking over his shoulder,

"How long have you been up?"

Casey (smirk on his face): *"I sleep lightly."*

They grab the rest of their belongings and plan their day. They went off trying to find their way to Russia. It will be a significant challenge. They had been walking for a day and a half when they noticed something up ahead; it was a road. They walk closer looking harder. It was white pure white, it was snow, like someone had laid a white blanket over a patch of grass. The glare of the sun on a slightly chilly day makes it look like it was a patch of ice. The day is going by so fast; light is turning to dark rather quickly.

Casey (looks at his surroundings, turns around looks at Chase): *"We are in Dzembronya. I remembered the mission I was a part of here. I can never forget this area."*

Chase (sympathetic): *"Would you like to talk about it?"*

"I don't need to talk about what happened. It was a long time ago. Do you think they know we are missing back home?"

"How would they? We are on a mission!"

Walking through the wooded area. They come up on a little house with chickens and pigs.

Casey (yelling): *"Tresser, are you here?"*

A young lady comes out smiling. She looks twice, and then the smile disappears.

Young Lady: *"What can I help you with?"*

"Tresser, how are you?"

Still, she looked at him like he was a stranger.

Chase (walks in between them): *"Ma'am, can you help us?"*

"It depends on what it is."

"Can you tell us where we are?"

"Wow, you don't know where you are. Well, welcome to Dzembronya. Tell me what I can do for you?"

"Can you help us get close to the Russian border?"

Tresser walks past Casey like he is no one.

Casey (grabs her shoulder): *"I am sorry you feel as though I never came back for you. The thing is, I didn't know where you had gone. When I came back, I couldn't find you. I felt as though you didn't want to be found, so I went back home to live my quiet life. This doesn't mean I forgot about you because I didn't."*

Tresser (continues walking and comes back with some keys): *"I can take you a little bit farther than the border. I'm heading to Voronezh, Russia. I can drop you off there."*

"Casey, what's going on with her? She doesn't even sound like she's from this country."

"She's not...Tresser was born in Russia. The very same place she has offered to take us."

"Do you think it's a good idea for Tresser to go to Russia?"

"Why wouldn't it be? We will be fine."

Chase had this funny feeling that something was going to go wrong. The beautiful woman was brunette, blue-eyed, just gorgeous, and had abs for days. Her nails were superb and she wore just a smudge of makeup on her face. Tresser did not look like she belonged there in that part of the country. He thought Casey was thinking with his pants and not with his brains.

Chase (walks over towards Casey) *"Hey man, snap out of it. I think something is awfully wrong with this picture."*

"What do you mean? there are no errors..."

"If you're lonely, I can set you up with someone after we finish this case if you need me to. Please do not get hard up on someone you haven't seen in a long time. Do you even know what she has been doing here in these woods Casey?"

There was no use because Casey's nose was too far ahead. No one can fetch him down off the clouds he has created for himself. They arrive near the borderline four hours later.

Tresser (turns around): *"We stay here for the night, then we come back early in the morning."*

Before they could get out of the vehicle, a man approached the car. Chase takes one look at Casey, and he lightly places his backpack up against the door with his gun pressed carefully up against his bag. He was ready for whatever came his way.

Tresser (looks back towards the guys): *"This is my brother."*

Chase was not taking any chances. He still was with his gun pressed up against the door. He nods his head toward the young man.

Chase (looks at Casey): *"You are playing right into this. This is to close Casey."*

Casey (smirking): *"You seem to think so Chase, but I am one step ahead brother. I see Tresser ideally manicured nails and her dying abs; not to mention her hair out in the middle of nowhere. You would have thought her hair would look disheveled, but it looks like she just had her hair done just yesterday."*

They both walk off to the bar right next to a hole in the wall motel. Casey gets out of the car and walks into the hotel getting two rooms. They both walk in the room with two double beds. The room right next to them is her room. Casey and Chase are wondering has the news got to Miller yet about the plane crash. They both were dismayed because there were no phones in the rooms.

Back at home, Miller's secretary receives a phone call. She is working late with files and folders covering her arms. She approaches her desk and looks over towards the caller ID as the name scrolls across the screen.

INTERNATIONAL AIRPORT

Before answering the phone, she sets her work on her desk.

Secretary (picks up the receiver): *"Langley, this is Miller's office."*

International Airport: {"Yes, this is the international airport. I am calling to notify Mr. Miller 00026 never made it to its destination. Can you make sure he knows?"}

Secretary: *"Yes, I would make sure he gets the message."*

She hangs up the phone and rushes into his office. Miller on a phone conference. He looks over towards her.

"Sir!"

He walks over

"Miller Sir., I have some terrible news. Flight 00026 never made it to its destination."

Miller (walks back over towards his intercom): *"I have an emergency, and all meetings are postponed until a later date."* (calls international airport, phone rings)

International Airport: {"Washington international airport, this is Amy speaking."}

"I am returning a phone call about our private plane 00026."

{"Hold, please. Sir."}

Air Traffic Control: {"00026 disappeared on our control system. We receive a phone call from Russia International Airport saying that 00026 never landed."}

"I'm on my way!"

He heads down to Washington Airport.

Air Traffic Control (greets Miller): *"Sir, a call came in not too long ago. They told me that 00026 went down somewhere in Ukraine."*

Miller called Attorney General, who made a few phone calls.

Attorney General: {"Miller, I will have a private plane on standby at International Airport in 15 minutes. It will take you straight to Ukraine to look for the aircraft that went down. You will be accompanied by ten other agents."}

They all are packed and are ready for their flight to Ukraine. They are greeted by their co-pilot.

Pilot (walks in): *"I'm your pilot for this evening. Rest assured this flight will be quick but safe. Buckle up everyone."*

"Air Traffic control this is 2626 ready for departure."

Air Traffic Control: {"2626 this is control tower stand-by, 2626 approach runway."}

Pilot: *"Roger!"*

The plane departs the runway heading to Ukraine. Miller continues his conference call to pass away time.

Pilot (came in over the intercom): {"Everyone, seat belts please. 26 minutes until landing."}

The plane arrives in Ukraine, and they are all greeted by the local Ukraine police chief. Miller and the agents walked in a big room for briefing. The Ukraine NSA and homeland all step over to shake his hand. Everyone gathers around the table with a map of Ukraine. The airport states the plane might have gone down somewhere in the wooded area rural parts of the country, which means that an area has to be located where the aircraft could hide without being seen. As they look over the map, Miller is thinking very hard and concentrating.

Miller (pointing at an area on the map): *"What about this area the woods?"*

Ukraine Police Chief: *"That area is a rural countryside of Ukraine. We can start there. We have enough workforce to cover some of that area in half a day. I know where we could land the choppers, but we would have to walk a considerable long-distance before we even enter the substantial part."*

Everyone boards up. Miller's phone rings. Alexa is on the other end.

{"Dad (she murmured) come home safe. We have a lot to discuss. There is someone I would like for you to meet."}

"I will be home soon as I can."

{"That is all I ask, see you soon."}

The choppers land 10 miles outside Dzembronya. They had homeland and NSA already out in the field looking for the crash site. The men were Miller, the Ukraine Chief of Police, along with three other men. One of them has a cadaver dog. They began sweeping the area where they think 00026 may have crashed. NSA and Homeland gave everyone their routes to take so that they could cover as much territory as they could. Hours later and there was no sign of an aircraft. Night falls and they decide to build a campfire. A little later, the fire was roaring and coffee poured throughout the camp. Everyone rounded back at the camp. NSA notifying all personnel they will start again tomorrow and to get a good night's rest.

Chase and Casey did not know a search party had rallied up for them. Stuck in a town with no communication, Chase dozes off, leaving Casey up. Casey suspiciously walks around town, creeps up close enough on Tresser, but standing at a far enough distance not to get noticed. He sees her talking to the young man who she claims is her brother. More cars pull up swarming with men and guns. It looks like all hell was about to break loose. Casey runs to wake up Chase and alerts him to what he witnessed. Chase already had one eye open when Casey walked inside the room. He had picked her pocket for her keys. He pulls them out and they both head towards the car. Casey got behind the wheel while Chase pushed the car discreetly down the road. Chase runs behind the car catching up so he can jump in. Casey picks up speed leaving behind Tresser and her crew. She looks back towards her car just in time to see Chase jump in after pushing it down the road. Her friends pull up as Chase and Casey steal her car. Tresser and her Brother jump in a vehicle and begin following them. After a few moments, they were riding up on the side of Casey, trying to push them off the road. Casey swerves to keep from receiving contact. He was driving on the wrong side of the street into oncoming traffic and came close to a head-on collision. He tries to regain control of the car when Tresser's friends come up from behind and ram Casey in the back. He manages to keep the vehicle from getting hit by bobbing and weaving. He recovers control of the car right before they were T-Bone. He pushes the gas paddle down to the floor. The other vehicle collided with a semi-truck and the explosion roared half the small town with a horrible shake. Chase and Casey were busy looking in another direction. A different car caught them by surprise and clipped the tail of the vehicle sending them into a tailspin—the car flipped over with Chase and Casey. The vehicle finally comes to a halt upside down. It is rattling from being hit and missing parts of debris are lying all over the road.

Miller (in another location): *"Did you hear that loud explosion? Can you give me clarity on that location? I bet you any amount of money those are my boys making a mark on whoever is messing with them."*

They continue looking for Chase and Casey. Ten minutes later, someone in a long-distance yells,

"OVER HERE!"

The Cadaver dogs are barking and they can heard in the distance,

"WE FOUND SOMETHING."

They walked upon an abandoned plane. Agents scatter the area looking for clues. The Ukraine Chief of Police notices the left side of the plane looks like 00026 had taken a hit. Before Miller can say another word, in the distance,

"HEY OVER HERE"

Miller, NSA, along with Homeland were walking up on three shallow graves. Miller, NSA, Homeland, and the Ukraine Chief of Police tells the rest of the crew to sweep the rest of that area. A phone call comes through to the local Chief of Police and the Chief walks over to Miller.

Chief: *"We found out what was going on in the next town. Seems someone made the local drug lords mad. Two guys have stolen a car, were joyriding, and wrecked it. I'm sending two units out there…"*

Miller (interrupting): *"I would like to take that ride as well."*

They pulled up two hours later. Another call came through to Miller. They found the little black box off 00026 and narrowed it down to the last time they were on the air. After getting power to the black box, everyone absolutely calms down to listen.

They hear the plane losing altitude.

The Pilot can be heard saying mayday repeat mayday.

{"WE HAVE TAKEN A HIT ON THE LEFT SIDE OF THE ENGINE COMPARTMENT this is flight 00026 we have some terrible turbulence. Our coordinates are 26*26'02.6W come in this is flight 00026, 26*26'02.6W 26."}

Seconds later, static noise is all that can be heard over the radio.

By the time Miller got to the site of the explosion, no one is in sight. Locals are cleaning up the mess of the wrecked car. Miller spots something and leans over to pick ot up. He believes that Chase left behind a note.

We are still heading towards Khibiny Mountain. You can contact the United States Lang Camera Inc. Company to notify Miller, our film Director.

Miller (reaches out to Attorney General): *"Casey and Chase are ok and they are still heading towards Khibiny Mountain. Right now, they are trying to find their way to Russia. Is it possible we could get a message through to them?"*

Attorney General: {"I'll make sure they know that we are aware of the letter they left behind."}

The Attorney General began making a few local phone calls trying to get a message to Casey and Chase. The next day, the Attorney General made more calls on top of calls to the Ukraine newspaper. He also sent every local newspaper a secret message for Chase and Casey.

Come stop by and apply for a job making easy cash. Ask for Ashley Scott at the job fair at 10:00 am following a lite lunch. Our location is 391 Neal N Court Drive Suite VA. Looking for two local good sturdy men with good postures and an excellent influential background. Job fair ends at 20:00 tomorrow morning. Tell your friends. If you miss this career fair, we'll also be in the next town making our way to Khibiny, Russia.

The newspaper came out the next day throughout Ukraine into some cities in Russia Rustov, Moscow, and Saint Petersburg into the Northwest countries of Russia. The newspaper notation was to ensure Chase and Casey would not have any doubt that they had back up when the time came for them to transport Dimitri back into the United States. Chase and Casey were making their way into the next town running from Tresser and her crew trying desperately to make it in Khibiny. They were causing a ruckus in the next city over in Vinnytsia.

Chase and Casey were in a rush, so they needed access to a car. They stopped in Bila Tserkva. Night arrived quickly. They both made up their minds to keep going to cover a considerable amount of distance. Walking with a fast-paced motion through a dark alley, Chase came upon a familiar voice; someone he had remembered from Georgia. That long Southern draw was distinctive. Chase caught a really bad headache just listening to her voice. He walks up from a dark cut on a gloomy night to a lighted area. He began squinting his eyes in disbelief. It was his cousin Michelle. Chase knew to tread lightly about his approach. He walks up like she is a stranger. Casey was envious, wondering who the beautiful woman was. He is thinking how Chase can get so lucky with knowing someone with a body like hers.

"Excuse me, ma'am, do you have change for a ten?"

The woman turned around, her eyes damn near burst.

Chase (knowing she was not his cousin that night): *"May I ask your name?"*

Casey (looking puzzled and murmuring to himself): *"I thought he knew her, but he doesn't."*

"Let's go. We need to find our destination!"

"What destination?"

"Wouldn't you like to know?"

"Oh ok. Now I see we are playing games."

She slips Chase a room number in a note that says

Wait for me!

They both walk off in the night heading straight to the only hotel in town. The young lady walks in and grabs Chase with a colossal hug.

"Cousin, how have you been?"

Casey (stumbling over his words): *"How are you? (before she could answer, Chase pulls her aside) We don't have time. We need to get as far away from here."*

"Do you even have a car?"

"Cousin, I need your car and some cash?"

"Yeah, I have a car. No cash, but I have my card. Do you need help with anything else, Chase?

"Do you have a phone?"

"Nope, sorry!"

(confused and babbling to himself): *"DAMN! What does she have?"*

"The car is a BMW rental. Please do not wreck it. I can't forget your driving Chase. Notify me after you are finished with it. I'll pick it up. It's a loan from my job. I'm working."

"It's nice seeing you. Tell the family I said hello."

Casey waited patiently until they were through conversing. He and Chase walk off. They had everything they needed except a phone.

"So that's your cousin huh?"

"Yeah Casey, and no, I'm not going to set you up."

They pulled off in a rush knowing they were pressed for time. At 0100 hundred hours, they entered Kyiv. They stopped for gas. Still on their mission, they pull off driving late into the evening. They made it to Bryansk even in Ukraine. Chase pulled out the card. They both have not consumed any food in days, so they stopped for a bite to eat. As they got out and began walking, they passed a customer. Something caught Casey's eyes. He spots the town's newspaper. He asked the man sitting could he have a particular section instead of getting the entire paper. The man pieced that section off and handed it over to Casey.

Chase: *"What is it, Casey?"*

"The letter you left behind in the car we wrecked. I believe that somehow Miller must've gotten the message."

"That was quick."

"Yeah, it was. Miller seems to have left us a message in this newspaper."

"What does it say?"

391 Stands for CIA, 1000 means the address for Langley and 7 pm Russian Time call Miller.

"Also, Neal is the street McNeal. Suite VA means Virginia."

"We have another ten hours before we have to make that call."

They had a long ride ahead of them. It was going to take them 4.5 hours to make it in Oryol Ukraine, and another four hours before they got to Lipetsk Ukraine. They were on the road all day trying to make the trip as short as possible. They made a stop in Oryol for a quick break. They drove up to a shop. Chase makes some purchases to get some money off his cousin's card. Chase and Casey made a phone call to the U.S. Langley VA stands by Miller, Attorney General, and Department of Justice.

{"We found your letter in the car you both wrecked. You both left behind much destruction in that small town."}

"Sir, we ran into some problems."

{"Problems?"}

"Yes Sir. We ran into Casey friend Tresser in Dzembronya; the rural part."

{"WHAT! What the hell was she doing out there? Casey left her in Moscow on his last mission."}

"Sir, she's up to no good."

{"What do you mean Chase?"}

"I'm not sure just yet, but she and her brother are up to no good."

{"BROTHER! He's in fed prison right now... and what happened on the plane? We have the crew bringing their bodies back home? We have a black box, but it didn't tell us much. We noticed the plane got shot down. The question is who targeted the plane?"}

"Sir, I spotted my cousin in Bila Tserkva. Could you provide her with a BMW?"

{"I'll take care of it. I heard your cousin is in a big case. We sent some of our men with her on a case not even knowing all the details. We need you all to stay in touch. Keep us updated on your progress. When you make it out of Ukraine, we will provide plane transport for you both in and out of Russia. I cannot stress you stay away from Tresser. If it gets difficult dealing with her, handle it then turn it over to the locals. Our time is of the essence. We need Dimitri back here. The court date is coming soon. We have an eyewitness in the protection program."}

"Yes sir!"

Casey (talks to Miller): *"Sir, before the plane went down, you asked me about a phone call."*

{"Yes, Casey, I was told that Tracy Fletcher was trying to reach out to you. I explained to her that she is not allowed to reach out to any of us."}

"Did you know what she wanted?"

{"No, but you will see her when the court date comes. You'll have your chance to chat with Tracy."}

"Thank you, Sir!"

Call ended.

Chase and Casey were making their way to the car passing through Tambov, Russia. Heading up Northwest, they are experiencing the real Russian side country as they go through the Rural towns and Villages coming from Dzembronya. Chase and Casey are going through the forest making their way to the next village. There wait is almost a short distance of 466 miles to Moscow. They reached out to the agency for airlift. They stopped along the way to gear up. Miller had them to stop by Russia's KGB. Miller has connections there. They walk in the house conducting the terms on the items they are signing out. Their entire business took two hours. Before they walk out, Miller's friend gave them a message from Miller. Casey placed the note in his pocket. As they walk out the KGB building, a man at a distance walked in on them both, pulls his hand out of his pocket holding a 45 Winchester Magnum, and places the barrel of the gun on Chase's back, nudging and pushing him.

Man (whispering in both their ears): *"No sudden movements or both of you won't have legs to walk on."*

In Chase and Casey's mind, all hell was about to break loose. He points them to the car parked just outside the KGB building. Tresser was sitting in the back. He places them both in the back seat facing her.

Casey (leans over talking to Tresser): *"Tresser, why are you doing this? I tried looking for you. I'm too tired. I have been traveling for days. Tresser, you're not making this any easier for you."*

Without warning, Casey reaches over, grabs her hair, boils it up around his fist, and pulls her just enough to where it is taming her under control. Chase takes his elbow and butts the man sitting next to him. The other man in the front seat turns around, kneeling in the front seat of the car, and places his arm around Chase's throat. Chase puts his hand inside the man's jacket pocket sitting next to him and pulls out his Glock 40 Caliber gun. He fires the gun busting out the back window. The driver stopped suddenly. Casey's body thrashed forward as he was still holding on to Tresser's hair. The more she moved, the tighter Casey pulled. Chase sees the driver getting out of the car running to the back and proceeds trying to open the back door. Casey secures the door locking the driver outside the vehicle. Chase turned and butted the man sitting next to him to his temple knocking him out with a light blow. He entirely turns around, looking at the passenger from across the other side with his Glock 40 Caliber pointed straight at him. While Casey still has a lockjaw hold of Tresser hair.

Chase (looks over at them both with a smirk): *"She likes its rough Casey."*

The driver was standing outside, looking in on what was taking place. Chase crawls over the front seat and pulls off leaving the driver stranded. Minutes later, Chase pulls over, opens the front door, and gives the front passenger a good shove, leaving him on the side of the road. A few miles later, the other man in the back seat of the car has the same outcome. Casey still holding on with a tight grip of Tresser's hair. Chase walks over to the other side, opens the back door, and pull the other man out. Tresser was screaming, kicking, and calling Casey every name in the book. She butted Casey in the face with the back of her head. She then greeted him with a smirk on her face. Casey pulled her head down with a tighter grip. Chase walks towards the front of the car and looks for something to tie Tresser down with. He spots some tie-downs in the glove compartment. He then pulls off riding full throttle toward Khibiny.

Tresser (yelling, kicking, looking Casey: *"You're going to pay for this Casey."*

"I'm still trying to figure out what I have done in the first place because you won't even talk to me."

"This is beyond talking!"

"Casey, we need to find the closest local authorities for your friend."

An hour down the road, they spotted a universal politsiya (police) station. They both walked Tresser inside. They notified Miller before leaving to handle the local paperwork. They left their badge info but nothing more. Miller dealt with the rest.

CHAPTER SEVEN
Mother Russia

CASEY AND CHASE were making their way up north, getting closer by the day. Chase looks at his mirror and notices someone is following them. He takes a right and they take a right. When he speeds up, they accelerate faster. After a while, the car turns off on another street. An hour later, Chase spots another vehicle following them. The car pulls on the side of them. The driver looks over, nods his head, and drives on past them. Ten minutes later, that same vehicle pulls over with the front end setting close to the stop signed. Chase and Casey pull up, stop, look both ways, and pull off. The same car pulls up behind them tailgating; as if they were hunting them down.

"I've had enough of this"

"Pullover!"

Casey steps outside the car and waits. The other car slows down almost to a stop looking them both in the eye.

"What seems to be the problem? You have been following us now for almost thirty minutes..."

The man in the car pulls over but remains in the car. He would not even get out nor speak. Chase and Casey looked at one another.

"What the hell's wrong with them Chase?"

Casey walks over towards them and stands at a distance. Casey played their game. He stands there staring straight at them without speaking. The local politsiya (police) pulls up with sirens blaring. The men drive off. Casey and Chase gets in their car and starts their way up the road. The same men came back around; passing them on the road. They arrive in Moscow with the directions Miller left. A Mi-26 halo was waiting in a field for their arrival.

"Chase, can you fly one of these?"

"It's been a while. Why do you ask?"

"I got this funny feeling that something's not right."

Welcome aboard. This flight is transporting you both close to the mountain of Khibiny. We have picked you both up with the possibility of one more passenger. Set back gentlemen, this will be a quick flight today.

Moscow is now 1900 hundred hours temp at 26 degrees with wind knots of 26 mph with a slight chance of snow later this evening. No worries, it is a calm day. Welcome to Moscow.

They had company on the flight. It was not one more passenger that was picked up, but four men tagging along. Casey glanced over at one of the men who looked familiar.

Casey (nugging Chase): *"Damn, we can't even catch a break.*

"What's wrong now?"

"Those are the same damn men that were following us in the car."

"Sure thing."

Casey (asking the men): *"Are you guys from anywhere around here?"*

They looked at Casey as if he had said something wrong.

"Hey my friend, I asked you a question."

They all looked at Chase and Casey like they didn't understand them.

The pilot had taken a hard-right turn. Casey nearly fell out the damn aircraft. Chase looks over towards the middleman who looks trigger happy. Air control was calling them.

HALO-26 come in repeat HALO-26 come in.

Casey (yelling): *"Hey, I think they are calling you. You're not going to answer?*

Trigger man glanced over at the other guy and tilted his head to the left. The guy on the left side got up and moved over on the other side of Chase. Chase and Casey look over at all of them wondering who is going to make the first move. The pilot took another hard right turn.

"If you take another hard right, you can plant me in between those trees down there."

The middleman attempts to get up. Before he could, Casey took and knocked him back down with his feet putting pressure between his chest and throat. The middleman grabs his rifle. Casey grabs the gun from the middleman and shoves it towards his face. The gun went off and the bullet ricocheted off the metal frame of the HALO as the gun fell to the floor. Chase grabs the other guy by his feet and pulls him out of the seat to the base floor of the HALO. His weapon slid across the base of the chopper. He tried to catch it but the pilot made another one of the hard turns. Everything was happening at lightning speed. The man passes Casey and slides across the floor with nothing to hold on to. The man pushes right out the other side of the HALO along with his weapon. Casey moves towards the cockpit, takes the back end of a rifle, and knocks the pilot out cold without a fight. Chase grabs the stick as he climbs into the seat of the HALO-26. He gets it under control with his knowledge. In less than thirty minutes, they arrived just outside the city of Kirovsk. Casey pulls out the note Miller left them and reads it out loud.

Dmitri's father knows you all are coming. Be prepared for what is coming your way. Trust no one.

They walk into town looking for Dmitri. They did not know his location. They knew their presence was going to cause problems. Casey turns just in time and notices a black SUV with a license plate, V. Petrov.

"Isn't that Dmitri's father in the SUV?"

"It seems that way."

Viktor Petrov was coming out of the Barbershop. They both walk over. Trying not to be suspicious, Chase and Casey walked into the barbershop.

Owner of Barbershop: *"YA mogu vam chem-nibud?"* (May I help you)

"Yes, me and my friend need a haircut."

Owner of Barbershop: *"OH, Americans! Sure, wait 30 minutes. Take a seat."*

The owner of the shop slips out to the backroom to make a phone call.

Owner of Barbershop: "Viktor, your Americans are here."

{"Keep them busy and I'll be there shortly!"}

Next!

Chase walks over and takes a seat. Casey looks around the owner's shop. He spots a picture of Viktor, Dmitri's father.

Casey (speaks loudly): *"NICE SHOP YOU HAVE HERE! I see you have many pictures on your wall."*

Owner: *"Thank you!"*

Casey tried to get the owner to talk about Viktor, Dmitri's father. The owner finished Chase haircut.

Next

Casey sits in the seat. Chase starts looking around and he spots a cabin with Viktor in the picture. The owner finishes up Casey. A black SUV with tinted windows pulled up with the name V. Petrov on the front and back license plate. V. Petrov steps out of the black SUV. 6'1 inch tall with a bronze tan, slick masculine body with his arms being the size of Jean-Claude Van Damme arms. He walks inside the barbershop. Chase and Casey are standing at the door. He addresses them both.

"Are you the agents that have been looking for my son Dmitri. I'm telling you as I told your boss Miller and the Secretary of State, I am not going to, nor will I ever give up my sons' Diplomatic immunity. Why are you here?"

"With all due respect, we are here to pick Dimitri ass up. He needs to pay...."

Before Casey could finish his sentences, Viktor's phone rings. In the midst of the conversation, the reaction on his face became pale.

He places his hand over his head. Viktor heads out the door, feeling distanced. He hops into his SUV driving off in a pile of smoke and dust. Casey and Chase look at one another with disbelief wondering what just happened. Local Russian police speed down the same road as Viktor Petrov did.

"I need to close up shop."

Chase and Casey were trying to put two and two together. They walk out of the Barber shop down the street into a luxury hotel. They grab a payphone calling Langley.

{"Miller here!"}

"Sir, this is Casey. We are having some sort of trouble here. It looks like all hell just broke loose again..."

Miller (interrupting Casey) {"Someone just kidnapped Dimitri. They are saying the Colombian Cartels. They took Dimitri in the middle of the night. There is no telling where he is now. Set tight while I make a few phone calls."}

An explosion went off just before the phone was disconnected.

"Sir, are you there? Sir?"

He heard a dial tone then the explosion went off. Casey abruptly hangs up the phone. They both run outside to check the commotion. Chase grabs his binoculars to have a closer look. He spots a man hanging from the side of a chopper. It is Dimitri with his hands tied. The other guy clutches Dimitri and pushes him back inside the helicopter. Another explosion went off. Whoever was firing was trying to bring the chopper down. Chase spots Tresser as well. He double-checks, focusing his lens on the binoculars making sure he seeing things correctly. As he zeros in on the chopper, his eyesight caught a glimpse of Tresser again. Chase rest his eyes from his binoculars looking with skepticism.

(with a long pause): *"Ummmm, Tresser!"*

"Yeah, she's in jail. What do you see?"

"No, she isn't…she's in the chopper."

"WHAT! Are you shitting me?"

"No, look. Tresser's in the chopper along with Dimitri."

Casey runs back to the hotel and places a call to Miller.

"Did you take care of the Tresser matter?"

{*"I did Indeed. What seems to be the problem?"*}

"Sir, it appears that she has something to do with Dmitri being kidnapped."

{*"What are you telling me then? Is she out of jail?"*}

"Sir, I guess she is. I'm looking at her as we speak."

{*"Casey, hold on!"*}

In Miller's office, he calls in his secretary.

"Can you get a hold of the local police in Russia? The same ones I was on the phone with earlier today?"

"Yes Sir, one moment Sir!"

Seconds later, Miller talks to the local police in Russia.

"Who paid for her release?"

Russian police officer: {*"Mr. Pastel Hernandez."*}

Miller (calls Casey back): *"You need to…"* (click, the phone went out)

You can hear static through the phone line as they listened to yet another explosion. Casey and Chase rush outside the door just in time to see the chopper going down into the forest. The black smoke was clouding their judgment of no survivors from the helicopter going down. Another explosion went off. A warm breeze went through the small town of Kirovsk, Russia. Chase and Casey knew they had to make their way to that crash site to check for any survivors. Before they head out, they made another call to Langley,

{"Good you called back. The phone had gone dead earlier..... Pastel Hernandez paid for Tresser release. He is the head leader of the Colombian cartel. He finally acknowledges his presence his in Russia."}

"Not right now Sir. Sir, the plane went down. Chase and I are heading that way."

The line went back out. Chase is looking through his binoculars.

"Casey, we need to move before everyone gets to the crash site. What did Miller say?"

"That Pastel Hernandez paid for Tresser's release."

Chase and Casey ran and jump in the car, making their way toward the crash site. They arrive to see everyone survived except the pilot. Chase and Casey made it before anyone else did. They parked their car deep inside the woods on the opposite side of the crash. They were running through the woods trying to make it there before anyone spotted them.

"This is an excellent time to tell me the story about you and Tresser."

"I met her when I was on a mission. She was in a little bit of trouble. She had owed money to these people that were coming after her. I paid them off but for some reason, they still would not let her go. She came along with me until I got to my destination. I grounded her in Dzembronya town where we found her, but she had moved farther out. I made a promise that after I finished, I would come back for her. I went right where I left her, but she was no longer there. I looked for her. It was like she had vanished. She didn't want to be found. I went back home and retired."

"I think those same people found her and she had no choice but to join them."

They stopped running, taking a short break, to continue the story.

"You left her all alone. She had no one to protect her. I think she did the only thing she could do: join them."

They hear voices looking for the crash site. Chase and Casey start back running. An hour later, they were still nowhere near the crash, but they felt like they were getting close. The warm air brushes up against the cold temp knocking the chill level up to 26 degrees. They take a 15-minute break catching their breath from running for so long. They were exhausted and taking sips of water out of their canteen.

"I am here to tell you that it is too late for your friend. She is working for them. Even though Dimitri is a criminal, she is holding a gun to his head. If we don't lock her up, Viktor will make her pay for this mess she is doing."

"Stop talking. We have to keep moving. We need every ounce of breath we can hold on to!"

They both started running, but this time at a slow pace. They know they need to hurry before Viktor and his men all catch up to them. They ran up on a helicopter blade that stopped them in their tracks.

As they started getting closer to the chopper, they spotted another module. Far up ahead two and a half hour later, they see the crash site. Sprinting the rest of the way, they walked upon a body part. As they gradually make it to the helicopter, they can tell that the pilot is dead. There was no one else inside. They are nowhere in this area. Looking around for more bodies, Chase found a wallet with Dimitri identification. Casey ran across three other IDs. It took me so long, but here are the files you asked for.

Was there anything else you needed from me?

"We are going to include Tresser. We have four people."

"They are trying to escape with Dimitri."

After going through the crash site, they move forward.

"What are you thinking?"

"Nothing, we just need to keep moving."

Time went on and they are still on the lookout for Dmitri. The night winter cold dark sets in and they need to take shelter before it gets too dark. The air was getting colder, so they stopped building a campfire. Later that night, they both fall asleep. Morning rose quickly. Casey wakes up and pours dirt over the fire. The noise wakes Chase.

Chase (groggy): *"How long have you been up?"*

"Not too long. We must keep moving."

They have no clue on their whereabouts or which way they should run. They started moving through the woods quickly looking for any trace of Dimitri. They made it Hibiny, Lake Imandra. They walked up on a couple of rowboats with Dmitri and Tresser. They are meeting a speed boat Northwest up ahead. They spotted a boating rental place, and after asking the owner how much, he paid with his cousin's card. They hop in the boat making their way upstream not really knowing where they are heading. They checked the boat in and paid for the rental on the return.

"Excuse me sir, can you tell me what country this is?"

"You're in Finland!"

"What the hell are we doing in Finland?"

Chase made a quick phone call to Miller.

"Miller, Sir. We are in Finland now. You will be able to track our whereabouts through my cousin's credit card." (gives Miller the card information)

Casey (ask the boat rental man): *Har du sett en kvinna med tre ansra man in sewdish?"* (have he seen a female with three other men?)

"Ja!" (yes)

The man points out the direction they went.

"Tack!" (thank you)

Chase got off the phone and they both corresponded on what each other found out. They started on their way in the direction given to them. They pass an ally where a man is standing waiting. He was smoking a cigarette. The man tosses it aside and begins walking behind them. A second guy, with a pair of dark trousers and a plaid short sleeve shirt with a light tone masculine face, follows them from across the street. Chase and Casey walked on the sidewalk. Another man, with a tattoo on his wrist, walks out from the corner with his feet propped up against the building. Chase and Casey slow down to a halt.

(asking the men): *"Them vad som verkar vara problemet?"* (in Swedish-what seems to be the problem)

The man: *"We speak English."*

"That's good to know, so move the hell out of our way!"

Chase (resting his hand on Casey's shoulders): *"Listen, we don't want any problems. We'll just be on our way."*

The man (pulling out a black trench knife): *"It's too late"*

The man was aiming the knife at Casey. The sunlight was reflecting off the end of the blade while Casey studied his attacker's move. With the knife clenched tightly in his hand, the dark Trouser man stumps forward. He takes Casey by surprise. Casey uses his hands blocking the man's every move from tearing into his flesh with the knife. Casey then twists the man arm crookedly by bending his arm inward towards the man's chest. The man stumbled over his own feet and fell to the ground on top of the blade to his death.

The man drenched in the smell of smoke came at Casey with a vengeance. The man kicked Casey in the chest with his feet. Casey falls backwards to the ground. The other tattoo man grabs Casey into a chokehold from behind. Chase came towards the Tattoo man putting him in a chokehold. The man grabs Chase's arms taking a deep breath as he grasps for air. Chase pulls him away from Casey.

Chase (asking the tattooed man questions): *"Who sent you here? Who are you? Do you speak English?"*

The tattooed man came at Chase with the presumption of killing him to the fullest until he takes his last breath. Casey was still trying to get the Smoking man to a halt to ask him questions, but he had Casey pin down. Casey raised his head to see a pair of long legs with stiletto heels on. He held his head up a little more and there were those long legs that kept on going until the top of her head was reached. A fire from a gun went off and they all stopped. Looking up and around, it is Michelle, Chase's cousin. The tattooed man and the one that smelled like smoke ran off. Casey and Chase looked at them in the position to run, but Michelle stopped them both.

(in an upset tone): *"ARE YOU CRAZY? What brings you here?"* (getting himself together brushing off the dirt)

Michelle: *"Your boss called me to see if I could give you all a little hand. It looks like you both need it."*

Casey (gets off the ground disoriented and watches this beauty in front of him): *"Goddess, what brings you here?"*

Michelle (looks at Casey smirkirking): *"Your boss told me that they found out where Dimitri is. He's still in Finland, but you all have to act fast before he disappears. I'll take you to his location, then I will be on my way. I'll notify your boss, letting him know that you both received the message."*

Chase and Casey were still getting themselves together. Michelle takes them to her safehouse where she has a friend waiting. She also gets her supplies or whatever she needs for her missions from the location.

Chase (looking around): *"What is this place, cousin?"*

Michelle remains quiet as they walk up to a steel trap door. She tells the man the secret code MI6 kaksinkertainen vaivaa (MI6 Double trouble).

Casey: *"Ummmmm.... Your cousin speaks Finnish?"*

Chase holds his hands in front of Casey's face to keep him from asking any more questions about his cousin.

"Uuugggggghhhhh......Casey, stop trying to be clever.....She would never be interested in you no matter how much you both have in common."

"Dammit, I'm your partner. I am not just any ole thing."

The door opens and Michelle walks in. She introduces Chase and Casey to her go-to guy for her weapons. They were led to another room with weapons on display. Anything you could think of was in that room.

Michelle (After gearing up): "Thank you. Put everything on my tap."

Go-to Guy (happy): "Sure thing!"

Michelle leads the way outside the front of the building. Two guys waiting outside pull Michelle by her arm. Another guy comes up behind Chase and Casey with a gun. The same two they released along with Dmitri's Father.

"Please tell us how we can get rid of you. Tell us so we can do just that."

"I'll pay you to find my son."

Casey (handcuffing him): "Extortion sounds good on your file Mr. Viktor. You would look stunning in strips."

"Wait...I tell you what? I'll waive my son's Immunity."

"Chase, make that call now if you don't mind. Time is of essence."

Michelle gives Chase her phone to make the call too. He calls Langley.

"Miller, Dimitri father is waiving his diplomatic immunity papers."

{"You all did it. Now we need to find Dmitri and bring him in. I'll get the papers rolling for you to being Dmitri Petrov in."}

CHAPTER EIGHT
Finding Dimitri

VIKTOR REALIZES THAT he slipped up and made a mistake. It costs him to surrender his son's papers. It was all they needed to haul his ass back to the United States. Michelle's work is complete after she shows Casey and Chase the whereabouts of Dimitri.

"I have one question... can you please talk to your cousin for me?"

"I can't promise you but let me think about it."

They walk up to the warehouse owned by Pastel Hernandez. Chase pulled out his binoculars. He has his sight on Tresser. She's on the phone; pacing back and forth.

"Looks like my Tresser is hanging in there. I can also see Dimitri is tied up to a chair with a gaged handkerchief around his mouth."

"We could leave Dimitri right here and let the cartels take care of him."

"If I was the one calling the shots, I would agree with you, but our mission is our job. We need to stick to it by doing what we were told.

"We might have a bigger problem... how the hell we are going to get him out of there?"

"I have a plan, but we wait until nightfall where we can have a better advantage in stealth mode."

After explaining the plan to Chase, night falls. Casey blends into the night with his sniper rifle, pointing at the main entry door, which Hernandez men are continually using. Chase blends in with the shadow and he takes cover. He spots two big propane tanks. Chase pulls out his knife and moves forward. He sneaks up behind one of the guards, and with the force of his hand, he slashes his throat. Blood rushes out the wound and the man slowly fall to the ground. Chase throws the other blade towards the other guard as the knife targets his chest. Chase pulls out activating a block of c4. He hides it underneath the first propane tank.

Casey (on earpiece): *"Chase, I count two more hostiles guarding by the second tank."*

Chase (as he hides the two dead bodies): *"Copy that!"*

Chase (pulls out his sidearm placing his silencer at the end of the barrel): *"Let's clean house."*

Chase begins to secure the area. Moving from his cover, he sees the coast is clear. He moves cautiously from the cover with his gun still drawn. He continues to blend into the shadows of the night to stay in stealth mode. He finally reaches the second propane tank. Spotting two guards by the tank, he moves out from behind, slowly raising his gun. The first guard takes a bullet to the head before the other guard could pull his trigger at Chase. Chase shoots the second guard in his neck and the man holds his neck dripping with blood. Chase walks over by the guard and fires another shot. Smoke rising from the tip of his barrel, silencing the man, without another breath taken. Casey spots a navy-blue SUV truck pulling up to the front door of the warehouse. He tries to contact Chase while he plants the next c4 by the third propane tank.

"I have a dark blue range rover at the front door."

"Damn! It sounds like the rest of the crew have arrived."

Chase raises his head looking for grounds to deliver his two fatal shots. He rattles a can in his hand, sending it toward the last two guards patrolling his perimeter. Chase needed a silent killer, so he decides to use his knives. The force of his arm was so strong that the throw was a quick one in the chest. The other went in his lower abdomen, clenching his wound. The man fell to his knees. Chase ran up in mid-air and sidekicks him in his lower abdomen. Where the knife was placed from the powerful blow; the man falls to the ground. Chase proceeded to the back door making sure the coast was clear.

"I am in the position. Are you ready?"

"Coming up from your six, Chase."

A loud explosion went off. Chase detonated the first c4 by remote. Everyone inside felt the building shake after the explosion, causing everyone to wander outside. Chase walks into the warehouse through the backdoor. He spots Dimitri tied up surrounded by three men with heavy artillery.

Chase (contacting Casey via earpiece): *"I need you. I have three men with massive artillery surrounding Dimitri."*

{"Gotcha covered Chase!"}

Casey delivers a bullet straight to one of the unfortunate men's chests. The other men scatter running for cover. Casey throws his last grenade. The explosion was powerful enough the men went flying five feet in the air and land on the ground with shrapnel stuck to their bodies. The heat singes their hair, and they have over 62% of flesh burnt beyond recognition. They both walked in, and Tresser is standing behind Dimitri holding a Glock 40 to his head.

"Do not move. If you do, I will give Dimitri what he well deserves."

"Tresser; you are not in control so hand him over and we would leave without harming you in the process."

Tresser: "What are you talking about Casey? I don't think you have the right or the authority. Just because you don't feel like death is not a commodity. I can kill him just because I feel like it."

Tresser walks towards the front door while still holding Dimitri hostage with a Glock 40. Nudging him in the back of the head, Tresser turns around and fires her gun right at their feet as she walks out the door. Dimitri tries to run and Tresser fires a bullet that passes his earlobe. She nips the corner of his ear. Dimitri feels a burning sensation causing him to hold his ear. He squinches his eyes and is filled with pain. He stops and she runs up from behind him, grabbing his shirt, pulling and nudging him her way. A helicopter flies over their heads to land, picking them both up. Chase and Casey run out the door, grabbing a hold on to the aircraft as it takes off. It was too much weight. The helicopter could not lift off. Chase falls but Casey was still holding on to the whirlybird copter. Chase is shocked and looks up at the copter as it rises in the sky. He felt he lost the battle having Casey's back, He sighs with his head looking down with disappointment. Chase makes a call to Langley

"Sir, Dimitri is gone again."

{"Who's gone, Chase?"}

"DIMITRI! He is gone… and so is Casey. We were trying to hold on to the helicopter as it was lifting off and it put too much weight and lowered it down. Casey's still hanging on. Sir, I'll be standing by waiting for your call when he touches down. More than likely, he'll be calling you."

Chase hangs up the phone. He wonders how long it is going to take before he hears from Casey. Chase started pacing back and forth. Dark rise, night falls, and still no Casey. Early that morning at 0300 hundred hours, he received a phone call from Miller.

Miller: {"Casey called and gave me the location. I used Michelle's card to get to the exact place. They're still in Norway. You need to get him out of there before Hernandez gets there. He was coming from Muonio Finland to Alta Norway close to the border of Russia. That is a four hour drive. You need to find a way to Norway fast; in a hurry. Here is the location 555 Alta Norway Island way."}

Chase: *"Got it Sir!"*

Chase took the night bus. When they stopped in the next town, he rented a car. He arrived looking for Casey and spots two bloody corpses. In his mind, Casey had already made his move. Chase hears a whistle blow coming from a direction. Someone is signaling him in their path. He spots Casey trying to get his attention.

"What took you so long?"

"I was delayed, but I was trying my darndest to get here in time."

"Glad you made it, Chase."

"These bastards are in for a treat… shhh, someone's coming."

They both are alert to what is taking place in front of them. Ready for whatever comes their way, two guards walk out the door, one of them holding a cigarette in his hand flickering his lighter.

Chase (walks up behind him whispering): *"Can I get a light?"*

The man turns around and Chase head-butts him. He then does a spin, wraps his calves around his neck, pauses to light his cigarette, then he twist and snaps his neck; the guard goes down. His buddy, the other guard, runs over towards Casey and pulls out his gun. He fires off a shot. He just misses Casey's earlobe. Casey turns around, and with the palm of his hand, he lefts the guard chin upward, grabbing him from behind with his neck placed on Casey's shoulders. With a death blow he snaps his neck. Tresser heard the gun go off so she walks to the window from upstairs. She brings Dimitri to his feet and pushes him towards the stairs holding him by his shirt. Tresser ties him up to a chair downstairs. She walks over towards the door, opens it, and looks around. Casey grabs a hold of the door; pushing it back in ans it hit Tresser in the face. As she holds her nose, she believes it is broken. He walks over and grabs her gun. She stands up taking one look at Casey and sucker punches him to his lower abdomen. Casey GRUNTS as he doubles over looking at Tresser with disbelief. Tresser walks over towards Chase. She sweeps her feet, putting Chase straight on his ass. He looks up, wondering what happened and who the hell could have done such a thing. He gets up, grabs Tresser by her hair, and pulls her to the ground.

Casey: *"I have never hit a woman, and I am not about to start. Please don't make me go against my beliefs. But do not get it twisted. If I have to, I will do just that. I will mop your ass right across this floor with no hesitation."*

Chase walks over towards bruised up, bloody, open wounded Dimitri. He unties him and brings him to his feet. Dimitri was tortured during his time with Tresser. They are expediting Tresser as well. Chase made a phone call letting Miller know.

"We have Tresser and Dimitri tied up. We need papers on Tresser for bringing her out of Norway."

{"We are not able to get air support inside Norway until tomorrow. Set tight until I can provide airlift. It won't be until tomorrow around 2200 hundred hours."}

Chase hangs up and relays the message back to Casey. He knows they need to move towards another location that Miller provided for them. They handcuff Tresser with plastic straps tied up behind her back. Dimitri was traumatized. He was not up for discussion. They place Tresser in the trunk of the car so they both could have a private conversation with Dimitri. Chase sits in the back seat of the vehicle along with Dimitri, putting Casey behind the steering wheel.

"Dimitri, where are the weapons you stole?

"I placed them at a private hiding stash."

"Your father turned you in."

Dimitri could not and would not say anything else. He just had a blink stare, holding his head down with doubt that he would wander back in the U.S., on the count of his father turning him in. They head towards his private stash to collect the weapons that he had stolen from the US government. Dimitri knew he would not be returning to Russia anytime soon. They pull up at his father's warehouse near Norway's naval base outside the city of Tromso.

The car stops. Tresser was yelling for dear life. Casey walks from the front of the vehicle and opens the trunk. Tresser had gotten loose. She leaps out the trunk of the car trying to dash far beyond their reach. Casey grabs her and pulls her back by his side. Casey decided to tie her up to the spear tire in the trunk. If she tried to get away again, she would have to run with the tire attached to her. He throws her back in the trunk of the car. Tresser starts yelling at the top of her lungs. Casey opened the truck, and she kicked and screamed more.

Tresser: *"YOU CAN NOT DO THIS; YOU'RE GOING TO PAY FOR THIS CASEY"*

Casey: (looks at Tresser with a mean look on his face): *"Like HELL, I can't."*

Casey gags her and places a handkerchief, along with some duct tape, to her mouth.

(whispers in her ear) *"Let's see if you can yell with this over your mouth."*

He slams the trunk down. Chase, Casey, and Dimitri Walk up to the front of the warehouse. Dimitri treads over then swings open the door to where he had left the weapons. He looks around but does not see any explosives. Casey and Chase entered the room looking at Dimitri.

Chase: "What is this? Where are the weapons Dimitri?"

Dimitri: *I left them right here, I SWEAR, they were here.* (whispering to himself) *"ya ostavil ikh pryamo zdes, kto-to, dolzhno byt', vzyal ikh."*

They walked over to where a piece of paper was taped to the wall.

Thank you for my weapons, Dimitri. Signed, Pastel Hernandez.

"DAMMIT that piece of shit."

"Calm down Casey."

They had no choice but to ride to the location given to them and wait for an airlift. Chase, Casey, along with Tresser and Dimitri, pull up to the estate with a helicopter pad and a field that was big enough to land a private aircraft on. They had everything they needed: food stock in the pantry and cameras for all locations so that they would not get any surprise visits. Casey walks to the back trunk of the car, slowly opens it, and he takes the gag off Tresser's mouth. He grabs her out from the trunk of the car. She spits on Casey

"You bastered."

He shakes her like a rag doll and places the tape tightly back over her mouth. He takes one looks at her with a look that let her know, in no uncertain terms, that they were going to have a peaceful night without her yelling. Then they both walked into the mansion. Casey slings Tresser on the couch and walks to the back room. Casey grabs a chair and places it next to her. He puts her on the chair, ties her legs attaching them to the chair, with her hands tied behind her back. They placed another chair behind her and tied up Dimitri the same way. Chase had perimeter duty, and Casey had cooking duty until the next day. Night falls. Casey accompanies Chase making sure he did not need anything.

"When we get back in the states, are you going to to let me talk to your beautiful cousin?"

"That's my cousin. She's not into guys like you."

"Well, what is her type, Chase? Maybe I can be that type..."

Chase ignores Casey and settles on watching the sunset behind the shed. Night falls and dark sets in. They both knew Pastel Hernandez had taken the weapons, and they needed to get them back. They realized that it was getting late, and that morning would soon set in. Casey noted that he will take the first shift. Walking around the mansion grounds, he was making positively sure no one could get in or out. Casey had one eye on his perimeter and the other eye on Tresser and Dimitri. As a new day dawns, Chase walks outside, relieving Casey for the rest of the morning. Casey puts things in perspective about how the hell they are going to catch Hernandez and those damn weapons. Morning came settling in.

"Did you get a good nights' rest, Casey?"

"How can one sleep with all this going on?"

Phone rang. It was Miller

Miller (on speaker): {"Good Morning. I was just wondering did you both make it there safely?"}

"Sir, yes we did."

Miller: {"Great! I also need to let you both know that the times have changed. The jet will get there in 1100 hundred hours. The jet will land 200 yards away from the mansion so be ready."}

Chase: *"Yes Sir. Thank you!"*

As they prepare, a car arrives at the gate. Chase looks at the monitor. A black car, with tinted windows, peeling down the road. The tint on the windows is so dark that it is difficult to see inside. The vehicle stops and the window rolls down. Michelle sticks her beautiful long tan narrow neck out and pushes the button speaking through the intercoms. She pulls up in a BMW at the front entrance door. The first person to greet her is Casey.

"What brings you here this early in the morning?"

"Your boss told me that you all will be leaving this morning. Myself, and my crew, need a lift out of here. Miller said that there would be quite enough room. That is why we are here. Looks like you could use some help."

The aircrafts circles around the mansion before landing. Everyone is ready. They all start making their way towards the jet. They board an empty plane. Everyone loaded up and the aircraft begins to descend towards the large evergreen field pointing west.

Good morning, glad to see you all made it. I am your Pilot today. As we head back to the states on this 16-hour flight, we are going to run into a few turbulences, but rest assured this will be a relaxing trip. Virginia's current Temp is 26 degrees with a 62% chance of snow, so buddle up, this will be a cold winters trip. Refreshments are being served. Your boss thought you all would enjoy a lite lunch. Again, this is your pilot speaking. Enjoy your flight CI-A26.

Dimitri and Tresser are sitting side by side. They both had a look on their face of defeat.

Pilot (notifies Miller): *"Miller, Sir, we are on the way in from Norway."*

{"Thank You!"}

Miller gets in contact with Dimitri's Father, Viktor Petrov.

The phone rings. Miller is asking for a conference call. Viktor accepts the request.

"How did that Mexican bastard Pastel Hernandez get a hold of the weapons?"

Viktor (smirking): {"Dammit, did he really get those weapons? Where is my son?"}

"Your son is actually on the way to the U.S., and he will be indited for treason and, God willing, any other charges he may have. Also, he will be put away for a very, very long time."

Miller's phone rings on the red alert line. The Pentagon is calling.

Pentagon: {"Someone called threatening all government officials. Pastel Hernandez is calling with demands on releasing his brother out of Federal Prison."}

{"What's wrong?"} (With a long pause, and a loud obnoxious laugh, Viktor suspends his conference call.)

Viktor felt as though he had the last laugh. He and Hernandez had this planned out the entire time.

Miller takes the call with the Pentagon.

Pentagon: {"Hernandez is giving us 48 hours to release his brother. He also wants Americans pulled out of his beloved country, Mexico. Within 48 hours, if he doesn't see any movements for his brother, he said the first missile will be released as a warning. The second one will cause a lot of lives to be lost. Hernandez explained that he has all three weapons and that he does not have a problem releasing them all for his brother's life."}

Miller (looking serious): *"What the hell are we going to do?"*

At that moment, Miller got a call from Val. He hangs up from the Pentagon. The groggy tone in his voice let her know that something was very wrong.

Miller: *"What a pleasant surprise."*

{"Yes, Mr. Miller, it is. I was wondering could I come back to work. I am ready, the doctor released me. Fit for duty, Sir!"}

"In that case, yes, we need more help."

Later, Val walked in and everyone was standing with applause for her recovery. She walks over to Miller.

"What is going on?" I heard it in your voice earlier when we spoke on the phone. Also, why people are going crazy around here?"

Miller was speechless and could not find the energy to answer Val's questions. The room was full of agents and the tension was so thick that it could cut with a butter knife. The phone rings again from the Pentagon. Val, looking puzzled, knew that phone only rings when the Pentagon calls. She needed to find out what was going on. She calls a friend in the NSA, trying to make sense of what was going on and why it was so busy. The phone rings on the other line as she waits patiently, calling a dear friend.

Friend Flocheart: {"Flocheart speaking"}

"Hello there. Long time no see."

{"OM Goodness is this, Val? I would know that voice anywhere. I heard about you being in the hospital. Sorry I couldn't see you. I am so glad that you are okay."}

"Yes, Flocheart listen, I am at work, and something is going on. Today's my first day back. Can you fill me in on what's going on?"

{"Sure Val, Hernandez stole those weapons that Dimitri had taken from the U.S. He was the first one that Dimitri sold them to, but Dimitri double-crossed him and took them from Hernandez and resold the same weapons to someone else, but he never returned

Hernandez's money. Hernandez now stole them from Dimitri bringing the weapons to Mexico, asking for demands on releasing his brother from Federal Prison. He gave the government 48 hours to bring his brother out or start he would begin detonating those missiles. It looks like you came back to work at a lousy time Val."}

"Yeah, it seems that way. Hey thanks and try to stay in touch more."

{"How about we both try that!"}

The phone hangs up. Val walks over towards Miller.

"Miller, Sir, what's the mission and where are Casey and Chase?"

"They are on their way home from Norway."

"What! Chase and Casey, what are they doing in Norway?"

"They went looking for Dimitri. Now they are on their way back here with Dimitri and Tresser."

"Who is Tresser?"

"She is a friend of Casey; someone he knew in his earlier mission days. She is very pissed with Casey for not coming back for her. While she was waiting, Hernandez used that to recruit her on his side knowing how she felt about Casey. Hernandez knew everything that happened during those years to Tresser had made her bitter and angry. That was enough for Hernandez to hire her. He was able to get the job done and now he has the weapons in his possession. I do not want to discuss certain events that happened in the past. When Chase and Casey arrive back Casey can go into details about, he and Tresser. There are some things that took place in the past but not ancient history."

"Yes Sir, Now I understand a little better. I hope he is open to talking about it!"

They are almost home, and Casey seems to have disavowed any events that happened in the past between him and Tresser. To be accurate, Casey pushed all that aside to focus on the task at hand. He decides to never discuss it again with anyone. His concentration is on the stars of all this chaos. He thought all of this was a hell of a price to pay for Dimitri. Hernandez, and his men, are going to pay for the betrayal.

The Secretary of State stops by to congratulate Casey and Chase on a job well done for catching Dimitri Petrov. Miller gets a phone call from his daughter.

{"Hey, what about that dinner you had promised me?"}.

Miller (lets her down gently): *"Can it please wait? I am in the middle of a lot of pandemonium at work."*

{"Well, when would he be able to see me....and could mother come as well? I have something important to discuss with you."}

"I will try and make it later tonight, but no promises. Switching topics, I need a favor from you. Can you find out Pastel Hernandez location? We think he is in Mexico somewhere." Alexa: {"Sure thing...I will investigate the whereabouts of Hernandez. You just try your best to make it tonight."}

The red alert phone rings. The Pentagon is calling. Miller picks up.

Pentagon: {"An explosion went off and two cars got bombed inside the Pentagon parking lot. We received an email of various scandal videos of unfaithful husbands and wives at the agency with their lovers coming out in the public."}

Miller (offering a final thoughts): "There is not one that Hernandez would not kill. None of these methods are too brutal or demeaning for him."

Pentagon: {"There wasn't a pattern to his madness, but he just wants his brothers' freedom and money. The money needs to be in an account. The number came along with the video. It also had a very brief letter attached."}

If we do not receive the money within 12 hours, the video will leak out to the public.

The SUVs came in with Chase and Casey finally arriving at Langley. Tresser was making an ass of her self-kicking and yelling in Bulgarian language. Dimitri came in with mistrust and looking strayed as ever.

"Tresser is speaking in Bulgarian; I thought you told me she's from Russia?"

"She is from Russia, but her father is forming Bulgarian, so she speaks three languages."

They place them both in separate cells far apart from each other. Miller walks in from the phone call he has been on. Hernandez was steering up a lot of shit right now. He is asking for two and a half million dollars for the videos that he has in his possession. The phone conference was into gave a lot of information. Consuls, vice-consuls, politicians, and even the highest social officials all were affected by this sexual video that might be released. They need to come up with a plan. The circumstances remain and those who are accused will be affected. Miller was between a rock and a hard place. With the help of Alexa, he found out that Hernandez is no longer in Mexico, but in Atlanta, Georgia. His reputation precedes him. He has made his way down south. If Hernandez is in the south, he is up to no good. He is in the right spot to fire that weapon off in the Colombian territory. They need some eyes on him so Miller rushes to find Casey.

"Casey, we need to talk. I know that you and Chase have worked your asses off. Have you talk to Tresser about Hernandez?"

"I have had the chance to, but I did not."

"Well, you need to have that talk with her. Only she can identify him."

They both decide in the interrogation room. They bought Tresser up in handcuffs and put her in the chair. Casey and Miller Walk in.

"Tresser, do you know why you're here?"

"Go screw yourself!"

"Listen, we don't have time for this. Your lover Hernandez has the missiles. We need them before he hurts a lot of people. I have one question. Are you in or out? If you're out, I can take you straight to prison. We don't even need a trial. You can easily get fifteen to twenty years. If you help us, I can get you off with at least two years minimum. Pick or I will pick for you."

"I choose to help the CIA."

"Wise choice!"

They release Tresser out on her on recognizance. Miller assigned her in Casey's custody while Chase stays trying to drop the money off. They take a C-130 from Virgina to Savannah Georgia.

"Tresser, I don't know what I did to you, but I just wanted you to know that I did come back for you. I looked for you everywhere, including your parents' home. I even talked to your brother before he got locked up."

"That's incredible, but what kind of man would leave without a word. Casey, I looked everywhere you were, and YOU were nowhere to be found.

It took me months to get over you. Now, want you to come back FIVE YEARS LATER, trying to talk so you say. You accidentally found me. You didn't come back in Ukraine looking for me. You see, we had this planned months ago. Everything played out just the way we planned it."

"What do you mean all of this played out the way you all planned it? Tell me what is really going on between you and Hernandez?"

Tresser: *"That is up to you to figure out Mr. Casey!"*

They arrived on the Army base in Savannah Georgia. The CI-A26 was on standby with further notification on taking them into Atlanta Georgia. Before they could leave Savannah, they were told by the pilot that they were having a little engine problem. The wait time was six hours so they had time to walk around Savannah down town area. They ran into Big Ronnie eating at a restaurant. He is in town making his deliveries. Big Ronnie asked them to join him. The tab was on him. He discussed with them that he has a meeting with Hernandez tomorrow.

Big Ronnie: *"I heard he is on your most wanted."*

"Yes he is, you don't want to involve yourself with him, you could get into trouble even treason maybe, that'll look bad for your image; Val's as well."

The waitress came with their order. She placed a plate of red rice, fried chicken, with mac-n- cheese for dinner; a true southern food. Tresser never had this type of food before. This was something new to her. Casey tried to show her that he cares, and he really wants to know what happened. He wondered how Hernandez got his claws into this angelica beautiful spirit. Casey watches her eat like he was watching over a lost creature. She glanced over towards him.

"What the hell is wrong with you?"

Casey went from smiling to a bitter zero. That angelica spirit is gone. Hernandez has robbed her of her delicate soul. It brought him back down to reality of the one that sucker punched him and called him a bastard.

Big Ronnie (calls for the waiter's attention) More *sweet tea please.* "Smirking talking to Casey and Tresser) So *you both were in a relationship before?*

"Who the hell you are asking?"

Before he could even get a word out

"Mind your own damn business Mr. Big Nasty!"

Casey mind was vehement with wanting to knock some since into Tresser's head, but it would be of no use. That beautiful spirit he knew was long gone. Casey thanked Big Ronnie for dinner and then he excused Tresser and himself. They go walking on the river bay but are very cautious of their surroundings. She looks distracted; like she saw a ghost. Casey immediately inquired what was wrong. Her mouth kept closed. Someone came over and knocked Casey in the head causing him to blackout. He was dragged inside of a black smoke tinted window Mercedes.

CHAPTER NINE

The Southern Target

CASEY HAS BEEN kidnapped. Tresser is holding on to Hernandez.

"You made it. What happened to you in Norway? You came in and got the weapons, but you never went to the location like we had planned on doing to have a talk with Dimitri."

Hernandez (laughing): *"Why should I when I have you? See you are no more to me than just a pasty; someone I can use to any extent."*

Tresser's eyes open seeing Hernandez for who he really is. She has been deceived by a man whom she thought cared about her. She holds her head down not with defeat but with anger; something she can use to whip Hernandez ass with.

She calls him by putting strong emphasis on his name. As he turns around, she knocks him so hard that he flew up in the air and lands on the ground. Making a mighty grunt, he got the wind knocked out of him. He grabbed her face and squeezed it so tight she started turning red. Tresser boiled up her fist and hit him below his waist. Hernandez boils up like a child in pain. She then grabbed his neck, bent it backward, and chopped him in his throat. He grabs her calves and pulls her legs from underneath her. Tresser fell to the ground on her butt. She was trying to rub the soreness from her butt falling on the cobblestone. She damn near broke her ass. She tries to get up, but the pain would not let her. Hernandez ties her up to the chair.

"I guess you're not going to play nice, and you don't want to be with the team anymore. So Be It!"

He picked her up. Tresser's face had turned red from the lack of blood flowing through her ass cheeks. She was in shock and deeply in pain. Tresser felt like she could not approach Hernandez. He has broken the trust between her and Him. He is not going to believe anything coming out of her mouth. He knew whatever she would say could be no more than a trap for him. Patel Hernandez is convinced that she does not give a damn about what he is trying to do. That leaves her only chance is to really try to work side by side with the CIA. She wonders, as he comes back to reality, where that would leave her. He walks over to Tresser.

"I just want everything out in the clear. Let's be frank. I know you were all into me, but I was into what you could do for me. I am not sorry I hurt you. Grow up. You want to play with the big boys so play with us then. I hope you understand, but if you don't, it makes me not mind. I have what I want..."

Before he could finish, his phone rang. It's Big Ronnie.

{"What's up? I'm wondering are we still meeting tomorrow in Atlanta."}

"I have a little delay. I am taking care of a business matter."

{"Well, I can meet up with you anywhere. I made a stop here in Savannah dropping off a delivery..."}

Before he could finish Hernandez interrupted him

"Did you just say Savannah, as in Savannah, Georgia?"

{"Yeah, I'm here making a delivery."}

"My…….My, this is a coincidence. I'm here as well. How about we meet at Inland breeze for a Caribbean meal."

{"I just had dinner, but I can stop by for a few Mimosa drinks."}

Later, they meet up to discuss business. Big Ronnie pulls up with the melody of Caribbean music playing in the background. He walks inside and is greeted by Hernandez guards checking him for weapons.

"You can never be too careful with this type of business. I have to proceed with caution. NO Disrespect aye."

"None taken."

Hernandez (walks up to Big Ronnie, shakes his hand): *"My friend, would you like to do some business together?"*

"What kind of business are we talking about?"

"My friend, see, I'm trying to take over the Colombian Cartels. I want all their shipments. This operation is bigger than I thought. Me and my brother want to be able to handle this by ourselves, but it is too much. I know that Blaze has his hands full these days, but I thought about you, and I thought I would ask."

"I like the fact you asked. I'm the owner of my own dock down south of Miami. I tell you what, I am not interested, but I will allow you to use my docks down in the south of Miami: for a cut of course."

"How much are we talking?"

"I'm not going to be greedy. 25% will do the trick.

"Sounds like a deal. Now sense we are business partners; I'll draw up the contract."

Hernandez orders his food and drinks for both!

Big Ronnie excuses himself to make a phone call to his secretary to draw up the paperwork. He ended up making two calls. The first is to Val letting her know what is going down and his location. Then he called his secretary getting the papers ready; with a clause in it of course. In fine print the clause states that if he misses one payment, Big Ronnie was allowed to take over his little franchise. Hernández was a smart man but dumb as a bat when it came to handling the business department. Pastel signed the paperwork they shook hands. As Big Ronnie walks away after having his Mimosa's he gets on back on his phone with Val.

{"Hey Ronnie."}

"Val, I did not have long to talk earlier, but I've seen Casey here in Savannah walking around."

{"That's strange. Tresser and Casey took a flight to Atlanta Georgia looking for Pastel Hernandez."}

"Well, he is here. I saw him earlier in the downtown area."

{"I thought you was in Atlanta already coming from Savannah."}

"Yes, I went for an early dinner before leaving and ran into Casey and Tresser."

Val knew that didn't sound right; she knew Big Ronnie wouldn't lie. He told him thanks and hung up. She told Miller what she found out. Miller called the pilot. The pilot confirmed that they were having engine problems and that they got grounded for six hours. Miller made a phone call to Casey but got no answer. Casey has a two-hour window reporting back to the CI-A26. If he does not make it there, then the mission has been compromised.

Big Ronnie spots Hernandez coming out of Island Breeze. He decided to wait and follow him. He winds up by the ports. Hernandez waits, sitting in his car tucked off in a dark alley.

Two hours had already passed and gone. The Pilot made a phone call back at Langley. He notifies Miller that Tresser and Casey have not reported back to CI-A26. A Conference meeting was needed. Val and Chase were called into the office. A call came in from a good resource that thinks Casey mission has been blown. They need to make their way down south. The Pilot was heading back that way. Miller needed them already to leave.

Val receives a phone call from Big Ronnie.

{"Val, I'm down here on the Port. Hernandez has a wearhouse here. He has been in there now for two hours."}

"Ronnie, do you think you can stay until we get there to make sure he doesn't leave with Casey and Tresser?"

{"I'll do the best I can, no worries."}

Big Ronnie sits waiting on the CIA and spots a lady running for her life with a man running behind her. She was crying like her life depended on it. The young man runs behind her, grabs her, and takes her back inside the warehouse. He thought that must be Tresser, but his distance was far, and night had fallen. He could not tell if it was her or not, but he still waited for the CIA.

The plane made it back to Viginia picking up Val, Chase, and Miller, along with ten other agents. The local Marshall's were waiting when they touched down at the main gate on Post. Big Ronnie called Val to let her know that he saw a young lady running outside the building that looked like Tresser. Ronnie spotted Hernandez walking out of the building along with his guards. They all piled up in two cars leaving the area. This was Big Ronnie chance to start snooping around, looking to see what is going on, and if he can find Casey and Tresser. Miller made a call to please release the two and a half million. He wanted to make sure to have it set up where it is pending in his account. That should by them sometime.

Chase (overhearing the conversation): *"What time? Casey could be dead right now. Why didn't you send both of us on the mission?*

Chase, I needed you here to have a talk with Dimitri, we finally got him in custody, and we need to play this smart. There is no telling what his father has up his sleeves. The aging diplomat looks harder than you think. When he speaks, he does it slowly, choosing his words carefully. He is not the man you think he is. Like his father, Dimitri is very smart, and I needed you there with your tactics for his interrogation. Make no mistake, Dimitri is not to be trusted."

A call came in before they made it out of the Army base gate. It was The Pentagon.

{"We received another phone call telling us that they see the money is setting there and that we now have 36 hours for Hernandez brother to be release."}

"We need to move fast. Val, call to see if Big Ronnie is still there."

Val called, but no answer. She repeated the call, but still no answer.

Big Ronnie looked around and spotted Casey and Tresser tied up. He spots a guard or two holding them hostage. Casey had a black hood over his head. Tresser giving them hell.

"Tresser, are you okay?"

Why did you ask Casey? You never cared about me before. If you did, you wouldn't have given up so fast on trying to find me. You continued living your life like I was something in the past and not in your future. I've moved to Casey. It's time for you to do the same."

"In that case, I hope we can be friends."

"Be what? FRIENDS! I think not. Will I take a break by being your friend? Can you tell me would they still lock me up?"

Val, Chase and Miller showed up just in time. Big Ronnie walked out towards them telling them he spotted Casey and Tresser inside and so far all he saw was two guards with machine guns. They all crowded the perimeter. They burst in coming from every location throughout the building. Hernandez was looking from afar. All this was playing right into his hands to see who he was dealing with. Hernandez made a phone call.

"I need for you to let off some bombs around the Pentagon. Oh, and make it massive!"

The call ended. Miller, Val, and Chase were able to get inside the warehouse just in time to get Casey and Tresser. Big Ronnie made a clean break without anyone seeing him. Hernandez also gets away. It looks like they needed to let Hernandez brother go. With only 32 hours left, that does not give them much time to get a hold on his location. He could be anywhere in Savannah. Miller figured maybe if they talk to Big Ronnie, it could really give them more information on what are his next plans. Miller talked to Val on the side asking her could she talk to Big Ronnie about Hernandez's finding out what are Hernandez plans and to try to find out why does he want his brother out of Prison at this time. Casey complained about a severe headache. They stopped by the hospital; they checked him out and released him in a matter of minutes. They were able to get back on Post sooner than they thought. Miller got a phone call from the Pentagon.

The Pentagon: [We have been hit with multiple bombs outside in the parking lot..."}

Miller had to place them on hold when another call came through from Langley.

{"Some kind of device was just detonated close by enough to make the entire building tremble. This is the work of Hernandez. He is saving those missiles in case he really has to use them. We need to find a way to bring him out of hiding."}

Miller (putting both calls on hold): *"Val, I need for you to find out everything you can about Hernandez."*

Before a word could come out of her mouth, Tresser had already spoken up.

"Sir, I know of someone you can use. Hernandez has a sister. She has a business right here in Savannah. She goes by the name of Angelica Hernandez Garcia. She moved from Mexico to help set up shop so Hernandez could run his drugs in and out of here down to Miami."

Chase: *"This shit just keeps getting better. So now what are we going to do? If it's not the weapons, it's those damn drugs. On another note, Boss, shouldn't you be calling your daughter for that dinner you promised her?"*

"Dinner, I promised her? "Oh Dammit...jeezz. I cannot deal with that right now!"

Miller (puts other calls on hold and makes a phone call to his daughter): "I am sorry to let you know that I won't be able to make it tonight. Could I get a raincheck. If it were not of the utmost importance, you know I would be there!"

{"Daddy, I am very upset right now. Only because it's you though, I will excuse it this time, but I need you to stop by tomorrow night and hopefully then I and you can set down and talk. I have some news to tell you."}

"Yes dear, I will make it my business to set aside some time for my baby girl." Miller thanks Chase for making sure he called his daughter. They are trying to find out what the game plan was by trying to have a talk with Angelica Hernandez Garcia.

"It shouldn't be a problem. They get along, but she's greedier than her brothers are. If this involve putting his ass behind bars, I think she wouldn't mind working with the CIA if only to make a way for herself to make more money without having to share."

Miller is stunned. He wondered why the change from Tresser. He really did not get to talk with Casey much to find out what happed, but it is killing him to find out what really took place.

"Tresser, I thank you for the info. I'll see to it that you get treated right while your gone for the two years."

"Gone where? This information comes at a price. I hope you didn't think I would just give freebies. Miller, you need to wake up because there are no freebies here. When dealing with me, everything comes with a price. If you don't know, ask Casey."

Miller turned hotter than the red stripes on the damn American flag.

Miller (addresses everyone): *Damn you Tresser... all of you, looks like we either roll with the punches on doing this our way or making a deal with Tresser so we can get that Bastard Hernandez and wrap this case up. To many people are getting hurt and killed for the sake of these two greedy ass men; not to mention families are being disconnected all because he wants his brother out if prison."*

"My na sdelke ili net davayte zaklyuchim sdelku ili net?" (In Russian language-are we on? Let's make a deal or not)

Tresser has hit the jackpot; the gold mine. She knew what she was doing, and the timing was perfect. Now she knew how badly they wanted Hernandez, and she was not planning on giving information without a deal written on paper. Miller got in touch with all the higher government officials to make it happen. They worked out a deal, but it had to be on her terms and what she wanted. She wanted her freedom and cash money.

Miller came up with a solution. They gave her everything except money. Tresser was not going to take that, but after Miller told her that they would put her in the witness program, her attitude changed. She would be able to stay in the US. with a new identity. Tresser wanted all that in writing. Miller secretary fax it in on board CI-A26. They all head back to the location and then head towards Skidaway Island. Angelica had brought her a whole island in the Marsh. The Island was gated; one way in and three ways out. Miller did not even pay any attention. He was just eager to get the information then get out there. They all headed toward the Island to have a talk with her. Before they could get halfway there, Tresser asked Miller to stop the car. They stopped along a wooded shack. Just before they got over the bridge, there is a tackle shop right on the river. Tresser added that is where they hid the bodies. All this is a cover up for when they have a shipment coming in, she pays off the coast guards for her shipment to come in. They parked the company cars. Secrets Service hops out the vehicles. Angelica had surveillance at every point so there was no area to hide. She walks out and the first person she spots is Tresser. With a smile on her face, she grabs Tresser and gives her a big hug.

"Are you still giving my brother hell?"

"No! Hernandez tried to kill me. Angelica, I am working with the CIA. Your brother is trying to get your little brother out of Federal Prison. He trying to take over the Colombian Cartels shipments. He wants this person called Big Nasty to help out."

Angelica (laughing): *"He goes by Big Ronnie. (gets serious) You are not telling me what brings you here to see me."*

"I told the CIA that you would help. I know how you work. I know how you roll. If Hernandez goes to prison, you will be able to take over what you have been wanting for far too long. This is your chance."

"Tresser, you're talking about my brother."

"I KNOW!"

"Hummmm, interesting. Interesting indeed... ... So whats the plan?"

With no hesitation, Tresser walks over to Miller.

"Angelica is in. Now, where the hell are my papers, because at the end of the day, she will side with me. If I pull out, she's going to pull out as well."

They knew Tresser had all mouth on her, but they also knew she would be able to back up what she was saying. Val phone rings. It is Big Ronnie.

{"Hey, just giving you a heads-up that Hernandez will be back in Virginia in a day."}

They had 29 hours left to let his little brother go,

"Anglica, can you talk to your little brother to see where his mind is. Maybe he does not want to get out in fear of what may happen to him. Maybe he wants to retain himself instead of making his time worse."

"My brother calls me every night. I will talk to him and notify you after he call."

They both hugged each other.

Miller (giving Angelica his business card): *"Whatever your need, just call me or if anything comes up, do not hesitate give me a call please."*

Angelica (nods in agreement): *"Sounds good!"*

Everyone walks off. Miller and Tresser go a separate way momentarily.

Miller (places the papers in Tresser's hand): *"The Marshal will be standing by when we arrive to the airport. May I suggest if you have anything you want to say before we leave. now is the time to do it."*

They headed towards the post getting ready to board CI-A26 on the Army base. Miller phone rings. It is the Secretary of State.

Secretary of State: {"Miller, what in the hell is going on? Bombs are going off, sex videos are coming out...our agents are sweating bullets trying to make sure whatever they have been doing behind closed doors doesn't get out for their families to see. Families will get destroyed. You are needed back here ASAP! I have postponed the Marshals coming to get Tresser. We need her a lot more right now and the government will get our monies' worth. She's not getting off that damn easy. She can enjoy her life after all of this is over. The Marshals will take her to begin her new life, but she has to help us out of this first. THAT IS AN ORDER!"}

The call ends abruptly.

Waiting to board the plane, Miller is deep in thought. He feels like he is getting chewed out in every direction. He needs to come up with a plan. He can admit they do need Tresser, even if he did not want to acknowledge it. He knew he had to put away his pride. He gets a call from his office. He has a call being patch through from Savannah. It is Angelica.

{"My brother has called. He discussed with me that Hernandez has paid him a visit there in Atlanta talking about some big plans he has going on and that he wants him to be a part of it. I explained to him what was going on and that the CIA was looking for Hernandez. I also tried to convince him that he would be a fool and try to break out now. (thinks for a moment) Wait maybe that isn't a bad idea. My little brother wants to help. Would that reduce his Prison time? I know the only thing I can do is ask?"}

"I will see what I can do. I'm not making any promises Angelica."

{"Like I said, all I can do is ask. I understand!"}

The plane just arrived back from transporting the agents along with Casey. Miller, Val, Chase, and Tresser board their plane. Nothing was said the whole time back in Langley. Miller was busy making phone calls back-to-back trying to put things in motion. He only had:

#1 the help of Angelica, who they would have to watch very closely,

#2 the help of her little brother, but for a reduce in his prison time,

#3 Tresser will be getting off practically scot free... Dammit, this just keeps getting better by the minute.

Miller knew all the wrong Dimitri and Hernandez had done. Everyone knows the Government wants them bad. Reducing prison time and letting Tresser go will be an easy price to pay verses Hernandez and Dimitri not being held accountable. Even though Blaze is in the mix of it all, the wrong Blaze has done might get him ten years easily; maybe five if his lawyer is that damn good. They all boarded the plane ready to take off. CI-A26 is up in the air Miller gets a call. Chase walks over to Val.

"Hey, I really didn't get to tell you welcome back, it's good seeing you. I miss the three Musketeers (gave Val a hug with sincerity) *I see you and Big Ronnie are still close."*

"Chase that will never change. He is my brother, and I love him. Don't get it twisted; he knows how much my job means to me. He promised me that he will never come between me and my job."

(talking with Tresser): *"I need you to know that the Secretary postponed your trip with the Marshals. He wants you to help. Since you're being a good Samaritan and all, do you have any problems with that Tresser?"*

She replied: *"NO SIR, I have never been to America so what better time there is in getting to know what's going to be my home."*

The plane prepares to land. 45 min later, the plane lands sign says,

WELCOME TO VIRGINIA!

CHAPTER TEN
29 Hours

THEY ALL MADE it to Virginia. An SUV greeted them at the airport. They had the Marshals meet them there. Miller addresses them inquiring who they work for. They told Miller the government and that they were there to pick up Tresser for the witness protection program. Chase and Miller drew their weapons; they were not going through that again. The Marshals called in and found out that the paperwork was void by The Secretary of State. They walked over toward Miller and gave their deepest apologies for the inconvenience; it was a huge mix-up. Chase called in and asked did anyone sent these US Marshals out on a case, but no one could find out if they really were sent out. Chase walks out a little faster toward the Marshals. One of them was still on the phone with his hand placed on his weapon. Chase studied him; he just could not keep his eyes off Chase. Chase turned around and yelled out for everyone to take cover. They all draw out there weapons running for cover. Chase runs behind a big green trash dumpster. Miller ran over toward the hanger, and Val pulled Tresser over with her behind the government vehicles. They figured that scum bag Hernandez must have someone in the Pentagon or the damn department of Justice. Bullet casing spread all over the ground.

Chase was dismayed because he was realizing that it was getting easier to be brought from other Third World countries turning against their own people. The very thought of it made him curse to himself.

The corrupted Marshals loaded everything they had into the SUV while aiming at Tresser and Val. Chase knew that Val had just got back to work. They are aiming for Tresser. They knew then that Hernandez was after her because she knew too much about his plans. Miller called it in; it was too much manpower. One of the men tried to make his way over by the car getting next to Tresser and Val. When Val realizes what they are trying to do, she guards Tresser like they have known each other since they were little girls in pre-school. Val directed Tresser to stay behind her knowing that Casey would never forgive her if she did not protect her from harm's way. Tresser did precisely what she told her to do. When Val moved, Tresser moved; they were like clones.

Casey heard the call come in the office while he waited for Miller and the rest of them. He grabs his keys, making his way out the door. Driving his Tesla Roadster, Casey pulls out of the parking lot.

Hernandez (walks out in front of his car): "All cards off the table. I want my damn brother out of federal prison. You all have 29 hours. In the meantime, within those 29 hours, I will be targeting Tresser until the government releases my brother from prison. Relay that message back to your boss please and consider yourself lucky. You could have been my easiest target I ever had."

Casey (frustrated and angry): "You are going to pay for this!"

Hernandez (walks off and makes a call): "Move out guys"

He gave the command. The man behind Casey nudges his head, he sighs with relief but angry enough to know when he had caught him off guard.

Casey (calls Miller): *"Are the guys still there?"*

{"No they are not? How did you know that they were gone?"}

"I will explain to you when you arrive."

SUV pulls up at the back entrance. Miller is making sure the perimeter is all clear. They all proceeded inside the old Langley building. Casey was hot and almost gotten himself killed.

"Miller, Sir, I had a talk with Hernandez. When all the agents were heading your way, that was his plan. He wanted to have a discussion with me letting us all know he is ahead of the game and nothing's going to stop him from killing anyone getting in his way. He also said we have 29 hours to release his brother, and within those 29 hours, he is going to try and kill Tresser until we release him. She needs protection. Do you think you can talk to the Secretary of State please? She needs to be placed in protective custody now, not tomorrow, but NOW!"

Miller (calling the Pentagon requesting the direct line to the Secretary of State): *"Sir, is there anything we can do now that Hernandez is targeting Tresser? Sir don't forget we have Hernandez's sister that is willing to help, but if anything happens to Tresser, we won't directly receive that help. We will indeed have an enemy from a very powerful woman. She is an ally right now and I would like to keep it that way."*

Secretary of State: {"We will do what we can!"}

Miller got an email with the sex videos that Hernandez promised them after receiving the two and a half million dollars into his account, which is a dummy deposit.

Miller (to everyone in his office): *"I see he is a man of his word after receiving what he asks for. His payday is coming, and it's coming sooner then he thinks."*

Tresser: (calling Angelica): "Would you be able to make your way up north? Your brother is into some deep shit. Apparently, he is not giving up. He wants you all brother released from prison right now. That seems like the only possible thing we should do now. Is your little brother still willing to help the CIA?"

{"So far, yes, but he wants some time taken off his sentence. Do you think they would reduce his sentence? We need an agreement in writing before he does anything!"}

Miller heard the conversation, and so did the Secretary over the phone. They agreed to receive his help, they decided to release him from prison. They made their decision jointly to let Hernandez's little brother go. Two hours later, the call was made, and Hernandez's little brother was released. Pastel made a call to inform them that he would not be given those missiles back anytime soon; they were his bargaining chip. He decided for someone to pick up his little brother.

They brought him to Pastel Hernandez. Before he left prison, he was told what his mission was and that his sister has his papers stating that they took three months off his sentence. He still had to complete the last eight months. They also made it possible that he would be able to get out two months earlier on good behavior. That was good enough for him. He signed the papers. Angelica made her way up north to help as well. She would be able to see her little brother as well. She had not seen him in five years. The plan was coming together. Before he left the federal prison, they planted a bug on his watch so they would be able to track his every move. They needed to have a talk with Big Ronnie to find out the meeting place.

"Hi, I need to know when and where the meeting is going to be taking place."

{"Hey, the meeting was going to be at my cabin by the Lake Tear of the clouds Essex County, New York, on the Southwest slope. You will need to hike it on foot to the cabin location. Make sure you come equipped because there is no telling what he has done on the path to the cabin. Hernandez might arrive there earlier than me. There is just no telling so be careful please."}

"Casey, are you up to it?"

"Yes, Sir. I am ready and able to do my job to the best of my capabilities."

Tresser decided that she would like to be a part of this excitement until the end. She traveled along with the crew. They all board up and move out for Big Ronnie's cabin. The hope that leaving two hours earlier from Langley would help them make it there before Hernandez. Just before they pull off, Angelica stops right in front of them. Tresser gets out of the vehicle and runs up to Angelica.

Tresser: *"Everything is about to go down. I'm glad you could make it. Have you talked to your little brother."*

"Yes, I have. He can't wait to see me so we can catch up just like old times when mother used to do our hot coco when it was cold. Now that I live down south, I have a lot of things I want to share with him. I wish you could live down south with me too. I am not as money hungry as people

think. I would give you a legit job. No worries with the feds or locals; just a plain jane life".

"You just don't know how good that sounds right about now, but maybe if I have a talk with Miller about my witness protection program, he could talk for me. I wonder if he could make that happen?"

"Just let him know that I would take care of the rest. It's whatever you need."

They all made a stop just outside of the town before they arrived at there destination. Tresser walked over towards Miller having a deep conversation. Afterward, Casey walked over.

"What are you both talking about over here so seriously?"

Tresser walked away, saying nothing much; just wondering when she will be able to get into the witness protection program. Casey didn't know what to say or how he should feel. He just looks her way, pleading with her to talk to him with his eyes and his sympathy being his words. Tresser looked at Casey without saying anything. She figured it was too late for them to try anything but just move on. Everyone got back to their ride and proceeded on their routes to Big Ronnie's cabin. Miller explained to every agent on duty how they were planning on handling everything from then on. They wanted Hernandez alive because he was of no use, not dead.

They arrived just in time. Hernandez was nowhere in sight. Big Ronnie walked over at a fast pace and told them that he had just called. He was five minutes away from their meeting.

Tresser (looks at Big Ronnie): *"Well now, if it isn't Big Nasty."*

Big Ronnie (smirking): *"You sure have a lot of mouth on you. I wish you would use that mouth to get my name right. Seriously though, I hope YOU need help when those bullets start flying. I will help you run for cover.* (smiling, he walks off)

"I know that look anywhere Tresser. You like him. (points her figures back and forward at Tresser) *You really like him."*

Tresser (bumbling on her words): *"Wha wha what? No No, he was just now being a smart ass, and what's the use? I'll be gone less than a week anyway."*

Everyone pauses in silence; they hear noise filling the air from what sounds like a helicopter. Once everyone spots the chopper in the sky, they all watch the aircraft as it begins to land in a evergreen field. As the chopper gets closer to land, the gust of wind blows around the area from the helicopter blades. After landing, Hernandez opens the doorsteps out. The pilot shuts off the rotors and the blades slowly come to a stop. Hernandez stops from a distance looking around the scenery.

Agents in there tactical CIA swat suits with bulletproof vests on are ready and waiting with automatic weapons. They were hiding in the woods where they can see the chopper insight. Hernandez and his brother walk towards the cabin with men outside heavily guarding Big Ronnie's place. Miller looks through his binoculars scoping out the perimeter as the CIA team waits for orders. Meanwhile, Hernandez and his brother walk into the cabin. Hernandez gives an order to his men. He looks back and the spots agents head towards the cabin. He panics and slams the door. He runs over and pushes a black heavy marble end table up against the door. Hernandez: *"Where did they come from? We need to get the hell up out of here, but they have us surrounded."*

Little Hernandez (puts on his vest and pleading with his brother): "Pastel, there are too many of them. I don't want to die like this. Pleeeease, let's live to fight another day."

Chase stands next to Miller.

"Brings back old memories of when we both did East storm tour."

"What can I say. I miss the action."

Casey loads his sig Sauer p226, Tresser walks towards him and gives Casey a hug and a kiss. He wondered what the hell was that for; a kiss of death or is it just her saying goodbye. He wanted to ask what it was for, but he didn't have it in him to ask giving what she might say and then was not the time anyway. That day everything was riding on putting Hernandez's ass in prison for good. Val walked over, trying to protect Tresser, she put her and Angelica behind an SUV. Hernandez saw his sister in the middle of this wondering what the hell she was doing here.

"Looks at his younger brother, do you know why Angelica's here?"

Little Hernandez (shaking his head): *"NO! What do you mean you see Angelica? Is she here? Where is she?"*

Hernandez (took one hard look at his brother): *"Are you both trying to play me for a fool? Are you both really this stupid getting me caught up in all this shit? My own family is trying to do me in... and after all that I have done for the both of you."*

Hernandez looks dismayed, feeling stupid and outrage that his own family would set him up. He does something that makes him feel lower than dirt. He turns the gun on his flesh and blood. Angelica tragically looking with her own eyes right at Pastel pointing a loaded gun at their younger brother. She looked so hurt and disbelief that Pastel would do such a thing. Tresser was trying to run over towards Pastel. Casey's eyes spread so thoroughly he thought he was seeing things. He realizes what is taking place and he tries to stop her.

"Tresserrrrrrr NO! TRE...SSE...R COME BACK!!"

A gunshot fires and she goes down. Bullets are flying lighting up the sky spraying every which way and loose. Casey tried his damnedest to get to Tresser. He takes one to the leg and he goes down.

Miller (looking right at Casey then telling his men): *"GO...GO...GO!!"*

Chase ran over towards Casey. Angelica ran over towards Pastel. A bullet catches him in his arm. Another to his leg. Pastel turns around spreading bullets every which direction. He was not able to keep up. His heart was pounding fiercely but his outrage was beyond his complacency. Hernandez had been betrayed by his own damn family; they turned against him. He did not even care if he lived or died. He felt when a family turns their back on someone, that person is dead anyway. His men came running over towards Pastel, pulling him away. His helicopter was on standby ready and waiting for him. Bullets are still flying beyond cognition. Hernandez takes off, wounded, blood rushing carelessly; he felt like he was dying. They flew him to a local doctor that is on his payroll. They rushed him in. Pastel was in so much pain until he asked them not to put him to sleep. He wanted to stay up. Hernandez wanted to feel the pain that his family put on him. He was wondering how he was going to get back at his own damn family, but he did not want to die under anesthesia. If he was going to die, he was going to be woke to experience his last breath like the man he is.

Miller calls in for personal emergency. He could not pass up on a favor that was owed. He knew that they needed help. They need as many paramedics as possible immediately dammit. He rushes over to Tresser. She's still breathing. He whispers in her ear to stay down. She heard him say the words. She gradually looks up, but not all the way. He ran over towards Casey. He was bleeding profusely. The medics arrived strapping Casey down to a gurney checking for a pause. The paramedic tells Casey that he is going to give him something for the pain. He gave him a shot of morphine and it practically slowed down his heart rate some. The other medics came in. Casey looks at Miller telling him to check on Tresser. They loaded up Casey and rushed him to the hospital. They placed Tresser and Angelica together. Angelica had to do something because she did not want to say goodbye to her Little Hernandez. Miller told them that he would explain later, they needed to take them somewhere safe away from Pastel Hernandez. Angelica kissed her little brother as he walked off with Miller. He places Little Hernandez in the back seat, along with two other agents beside him, and they drive off.

Miller gets on the phone with the Secretary of State. He calls in for a specialist for Casey. Miller asked Chase to play along with him about Tresser. Miller explained to Chase that he was letting Tresser go stay with Angelica. They needed to find Pastel. Miller had already talked to Big Ronnie. He says he knows of a doctor that is on Pastel payroll. They need to get to him while he is vulnerable and before that bastard disappears. Little Hernandez heard everything.

"I know of the doctor my brother uses. He is on Pastel's payroll and has his own private practice. I can take you there."

"You've done enough young man. Now that Pastel knows you and your sister are against him, he is out for blood. We need to take him while he's hurt."

They arrived back to the agency gathering up more men. Before playing their last card, they need to stop by the hospital to check in on Casey.

"Casey took a bullet to the leg. He will be out for about three months. No work, no sex, or no strenuous activities. He is going to need an around-the clock nurse coming helping him with his daily hygiene. He will be in some discomfort and pain, but other than that, he will make it through. The hospital also wants to keep him for one or two days. He stated that he did not want any pain medication until he talked to Miller. Miller was allowed to see him for a few minutes. He walks in the room and sees tears in Casey eyes.

"What the hell was that all about out there?"

"After this whole thing blew up in our faces, I the decent thing. All I saw was Tresser…" He could not finish as silent tears rolled harder down Casey's cheeks as he thought about her running into a hail of bullets. He knew it was Tresser playing with his thoughts, mind, and heart. He thought about when he first met, and her those memories just would not go away."

Miller (softens up): *"Awe Casey, we knew you cared about her."*

Casey: *"I knew her, that's why I feel like this. That bestarred took her away. He needs to pay for this sir. Hernandez has caused so much heartache in every path he has crossed. It's time for him to go down."*

The nurse came in, along with the doctor, to give him a shot. A few minutes later, Casey was out. Chase and Miller Walk out. Val came to the hospital.

"We got Tresser situated at a safe house along with Angelica. We also sent her Little Hernandez there for the time being. Sir, I just wanted you to know what I've done. I didn't want them separated for now."

"No problem. I need all agents on deck. We need to bring that Bastard TODAY! Val, call Big Ronnie for me and tell him that we need to know where Pastel is."

"On it right now Sir!"

Val walks off on the phone trying to get a hold of Big Ronnie. He did not pick up the phone. It kept going straight to voicemail. She and Ronnie were both calling each other at the same time. She places another call out. Still no answer. They were playing phone tag. Ronnie was pulling up at the Doctor private care facility. Pastel had called him there. Big Ronnie text Val letting her know where he was. He sent her the address to his location.

CHAPTER ELEVEN

Settling The Score

CHASE: *"MILLER SIR, Tresser isn't dead what are you doing?"*

Miller: *"She wanted this Chase, and I respect her wishes. Tresser told me why she went in with Dimitri and Hernandez. She felt as though Casey needed to move on and that his world is not for her. She will be leaving with Angelica going back south. Her ties will not be completely cut off from the CIA. She agrees that within time, she would become our informant whenever we needed her. She has sworn to help us out. The Secretary of State and I agreed with her, and he made this happen for her. We told Angelica that Tresser better keeps herself clean. No Mafia, No Cartels, No Drug life. She needs a real job. We are going to provide her with a whole new identity. She will have a new life, but if we don't get Pastel, then that will not happen."*

"I understand that Sir!"

Miller had a briefing on his earpiece.

{"EVERYONE LISTEN UP! This is going to be your conference over the earpiece so pay close attention. We have no time. We are here to capture one Pastel Hernandez. He's very dangerous. He shot one of our agents today in the field of duty. He also attempted to kiss his own brother so he has no regard for anyone's life but his. He has taken a bullet to the leg and his right arm. He is laid up in some kind of compound. Agent Val has that info Val."}

Val (over her earpiece): {"Okay guys we have a informant on the inside.""

Miller (looking over at her): "WHO?"

"Big Ronnie is there. He called me to let me know Pastel called him in because he needed to have a talk with him."

{"Continuing, as I just stated, we have someone on the inside. Most of you know him as Big Ronnie. Today is shoot and ask questions later, but remember big Ronnie is inside."}

They all piled up in the SUV's and they moved out. Val calls Big Ronnie. He finally answers the phone.

"Hey, what's going on?"

"Pastel is trying to get moved, but not before he clips his sister and his little brother."

"Dammit, we need to move out before he leaves. Can you steer him for us. We are heading your way."

"I can stall, but I can't say for how long. I mean after all, Hernandez and I are both businessmen and with that being said, it's not going to take long for him to figure this out. The only reason he still trusts me is because he thinks his family is behind everything and not me."

"Just stall him because every second counts."

Big Ronnie hangs up the phone. Governors SUVs rush through traffic with federal agents and CIA black ops swat team inside. They roll through the city streets with sirens blasting from each SUVs while helicopters are air born flying towards the destination.

Hernandez sets the timer on one of the nuclear missiles after he enters a pin on his cell phone. The missile shows 'armed' flashing across the screen. The bomb happens to be in the center of downtown. Hernadez then calls 911.

{"911 what's your emergency?"}

"There's a missile downtown and I believe it's armed. I'm watching 30 minutes on the screen. Send help now!"

{"Where's your location?"}

Hernandez hangs up the phone, rolls down his window, and toss the phone out. Then he rolls his window back up.

Hernandez (smiling): They want entertainment...they got it. Let's head down to the Ports. I need to talk to a friend about trust issue."

On their way to the Ports as well, Miller cell phone rings and he answers.

Chase phones rings. It is Michelle.

"Michelle."

{"Word got out that Hernandez has armed a missile inside the heart of the city."}

"The heart of the city?"

{"DOWNTOWN!"}

Chase quickly hangs up the phone and he taps Miller on the shoulder, who happens to be sitting in the passenger seat. Before Miller could reply to chase, they approach an intersection where bomb squad, fire trucks, and police officers drives by in a hurry. They realized the intersections were being blocked off.

"What the hell is going on now? Dammit dammit dammit!"

"Hernández armed the first missile, and he chose downtown as a target."

"The heart of the city."

"He probably knows by now that Big Ronnie is in on the deal, so his life is probably in danger as well."

"This is your call Miller."

"Chase, I need you to find out where is the weapon going to land at and handle it for me. Then meet at Big Ronnie and Pastel Hernandez location."

Chase was left making his way downtown. Hernandez had the hit heading straight for the old City Hall in downtown Virginia. Chase had to make it before the weapon went off. He needed to give the coordinates to the Armed Forces Pilots to disengage the missiles heading to Virginia City Hall. He makes his call patching him through to the pilot. He gives him the coordinates.

"37*32'23N 26*62'59/ 26.26666*N."

{"Roger, Sir!"}

Miller knew there was not much time left. They needed to get Hernandez quickly and in a hurry. Pastel told Big Ronnie that their backgrounds are very much alike. Pastel realizes his attempt was not successful. Pastel prejudged and he should not have done that. What he went through is far beyond anyone's reach. Big Ronnie felt that

Hernandez is having second thoughts but feels it may be too late. They meet up at the ports anyway.

"You're being too kind. Not being offensive, but too much has happened and kindness from you really freaking me out. Knowing where you stand makes me real nervous Hernandez."

"Big Ronnie, I have no one standing by my side. My own damn family is gone...they are dead to me. My little brother and my own damn sister even turned... MY SISTER can you believe this? I have given them everything. My friends, I also knew you were working alongside the CIA. I feel dirty. I need to show you that I oversee my own thoughts."

He raises his gun and shoots a round at Big Ronnie. He misses him from being so weak. Pastel gets up with a limp walking slowly toward Big Ronnie. What was going through Ronnie thoughts were no longer a reality. He is wondering what is taking the CIA so long. They should have been there by now. His thoughts had gotten distracted. He turned around and Hernandez was close enough not to miss this time. He fired another shot. It hit Ronnie right in his lower abdomen. He clenched a tight hold of his lower body with so much pain. He soon realizes that he never gave Val his location. Big Ronnie slides his arm up against his body trying to turn on his tracking signaling device. He figured Val should be able to pick up on that in his slow radical voice. Pastel falls out from the loss of too much blood. Big Ronnie was not strong enough to call Val. He fell to his knees and collapsed flat on his face and passed out. Ten minutes later sirens could be heard coming up. Val was leading them to his location. She gets out of the unmarked SUV and stumbles inside looking for Big Ronnie. She finds him passed out. She ran over calling his name and checking for pause. His breathing is very shallow, so she orders the paramedics for them both. Miller and Chase come walking at a fast pace. They walk over towards Hernandez attaching handcuffs. The paramedics arrive, taking him away to the same hospital as Casey. Everyone rushes over to the hospital. While they wait, other agents decide to see Casey. Chase and Miller walked in Casey's room, but he was in and out of it. They pass time in his room keeping him company. Feeling groggy, he wakes up. Turning his head around, he see Chase & Miller.

"Look who…wow my two fav co-workers are here to see me."

His mind is in a nice place of feeling good. He looks up at them both wondering why they are looking like they both must have had a shitty day.

Miller (looking at Casey): *"We got him!"*

Casey (eyes opening wider): *"What did you just say?"*

"We got that Bastard! He is here in the hospital."

Casey wipes his mouth. He was puzzled, but still had a smile on his face a smile of relief.

Casey (laying back with so much pride and smiling): *"We got him!"*

Chase (looking at Miller-walks over and whispers in his ear): *"Casey is going to chew your ass out for taking him through this. I hate to tell you Miller, Sir. but you haven't seen nothing yet."*

Chase with a smirk walked off with Miller looking directly at Chase.

Miller: *"Casey, get some rest. We'll come back later on to check on you."*

Miller heads to the office gathering up everything and making phone calls about court for Blaze, Dimitri and Hernandez. Court is set for the next day.

Casey was released later on that evening. Chase and Val both pick Casey up escorting him home setting him up to be comfortable. They both left telling him they'd stop by the next day to pick him up for court.

Val, still living next door, made sure Casey had a way to court. She walked to his door and was greeted by a nurse. Casey was ready for his debut. Looking stronger than ever, he made it to court. Tracy Fletcher walks up to Casey. He damn near did not know who she was. She gives him a hug. He was still in pain. He turned around and saw something he could not believe. He thought his eyes were playing tricks on him. He tried focusing his eye sight on what he thought was a joke he ...he..he sees Tresser. Looking baffled he almost tripped over his own wounded leg. Chase took one look at Miller and walked off. Tresser walks over toward Casey.

Casey (shaking his head): "NO...NO! (teary eyed) *Is it really you? I thought you died...*"

"*No, I didn't. Your boss helped me out and so did your higher officials. I'm leaving Casey. I will be living down south with Angelica, but you will get to see me from time to time whenever you all need help. I told you boss that I will cooperate whenever he needs me. Casey, I want you to take care of yourself and allow yourself to love. It was never going to work out between you and I, but that doesn't mean you should just give up.*"

A call came out.

TRESSER! You are due inside for testimony.

Casey (looks directly at his Miller-walks up and whispers in his ear): *You're on my shit list.*"

He then patted him on his shoulders and walked off.

207

Chase (looking with a giggle and a smirk combined): *"I told you he is not done yet."*

Judge in the background-hitting the gavel on the bench.

Court adjourned.

Miller heading back to the office gets a call from his daughter.

{"Dad, I have been trying to get you and mother here for dinner for weeks. I waited patiently. There is no other way of telling you than to just say it......"}

Miller (puzzled) There was a pause, Miller was hesitant to reply. He finally broke down

"WHAIT!!! I understand why don't we set-up a dinner date me and your mother one evening"

{"Daddy, I would love that. How about tonight. I have already started dinner you and mother haven't seen my new home yet. Dinners cooking ill just call mother and you both come over right after work."}

Miller (pale faced):" I'll *be right over!"*

Miller finally makes it to his daughter's home. She opens the door and welcomes him with a kiss on the cheek. His wife, Martha, made it and greets her husband as well.

Before Miller could get the last sentence out, someone walked through the door. Miller looks behind him and sees it is Chase.

"HONEY I'M HOME"!

Printed in the United States
by Baker & Taylor Publisher Services

Printed in the United States
by Baker & Taylor Publisher Services